SCARRED

SCARRED: BOOK 1

TT KOVE

ARCTIC CIRCLE PRESS

CHAPTER 1

DAMIAN

ur meeting was, in hindsight, rather disturbing.

Rain poured down, and I had cut across Soho Square Garden to get home quicker when I saw him sitting on the grass. His knees were drawn up and his face was buried in the palm of his hands. He was soaked all the way through, and I could see, even from a distance, that he was trembling.

He sat under a tree, but it didn't give him much shelter from the rain. The streetlight next to him flickered on and off, making the entire setting eerie. I glanced around, but I was the only person here besides him.

I reckoned that was to be expected when it was past eleven at night and the weather was shit.

Even in the middle of London.

I looked back at him.

I couldn't leave him there.

Not when he was so distressed he was voluntarily sitting outside in the rain clad only in jeans and a thin, long-sleeved jumper.

I walked over, slow and hesitant. He didn't move as I approached, even though he had to hear my squishy steps in the wet grass.

Only when I stopped at his side and held the umbrella out to cover him did he react.

He lifted his head and peered up at me. Blond hair, darkened by the rain, was plastered to his skin and his eyes, such a brilliant green they startled me, were red and swollen. I realised with a start that he'd been crying. Probably still was. I didn't believe for a second that all the drops on his face were from the rain.

"If you stay like this you'll get sick." It wasn't the best thing to say, for sure, but then I'd never been good when it came to other people.

He sniffled and ran a hand over his face. Not that it helped much, as his hand was just as wet as the rest of him. "I c-can't go h-home." His teeth chattered so badly I had a hard time understanding—but I caught what he'd said, and his words made me fidget uncomfortably.

I couldn't leave him out there. He'd end up with pneumonia or do something to endanger himself. He seemed distraught enough to be capable of it. I couldn't, in good conscience, walk away and leave him to his own fate.

"Why not?" I looked around again. There was still no one else around. "You should go home."

He shook his head fiercely. "I can't."

I looked around for the third time, more anxious now. It was getting late, it was cold, and it didn't look like the rain was about to ease up anytime soon. "Don't you have any friends you can go to?"

"No." His voice was only a murmur. "I don't have any friends."

I pursed my lips uncertainly. "You can't stay out here. You'll get pneumonia." I'd had that once, and it had *not* been fun. "I guess you could—" I cut myself off to swallow, hard. "You could come with me. I live right across the street."

He looked up at me, a strange gleam in his eyes. "You sure?"

"Yeah." I wasn't, not at all. But if I left him out here, and he had nowhere else to go… I couldn't do that. I didn't much like people, but I wasn't heartless. "Yeah, come on."

He planted his palms on the wet ground and pushed himself up. He stumbled a little as he straightened up, and I grabbed his arm on impulse to keep him from losing his balance.

He hissed and jerked away, holding his arm tight to his chest.

I stared at him, taken aback. Not just by him so suddenly pulling away, but because I'd grabbed onto him to begin with. I wasn't fond of touching or being touched; and I *never* initiated it.

"I'm sorry," I muttered.

"No, *I'm* sorry." He brought his other hand up to cover the one still pressed against his chest. "I've hurt my hand, that's all. So it hurts to touch it. You wouldn't have known that."

"Okay." I didn't know what else to say. I wasn't sure I believed him.

He was standing outside the range of the umbrella now, so the rain pelted down on him once again.

"Come on." I inched the umbrella closer to him.

He looked at me, a strange gleam in his eyes, then he gave a slow nod.

I walked as far away from him as was possible underneath the umbrella. It was beyond awkward, but it was only a few minutes to my flat. The door was locked and all the lights seemed to be out, which meant that Silver wasn't home.

I didn't know if I should be disappointed about

that or not. Silver was good at talking to people, whereas I was not. It wouldn't have been so awkward if he'd been home. Then again, how was I going to explain the current situation to him?

"Bathroom's there." I pointed to the closed door next to my own bedroom, across the room from us. "I'll find you something dry to wear."

"Thank you." He didn't meet my eyes as he shuffled past me towards the bathroom.

I watched his back, but when I realised what I was doing I shook my head and hurried into my bedroom. I found a pair of grey joggers and a thin, white jumper that I hoped wouldn't be too big on him. From what I could see he was a slighter build than me.

I hesitated for a moment outside the bathroom door, then told myself off and knocked on it. He cracked it open, and I handed over the neatly folded clothes.

"Thanks." He took them with a small smile.

I scratched the back of my neck as I headed over to the sofa. What was I doing? I'd just brought a stranger into my home. I didn't know anything about him. He could be deranged or a thief or a murderer. Any of those were just as likely. But he could also just be a sad bloke who didn't have anywhere else to go.

The bathroom door opened, and I tilted my head

to the side so I could watch him emerge. My clothes were too big on him, but that only served to make him look adorable.

I can't believe I'm thinking that. But it's true.

He *was* adorable. His hair was still wet, but he'd run his fingers through it to ruffle it up.

I resolutely turned my focus on the black television when he sat down next to me. I could feel his eyes on me though, and it made me twitch uncomfortably. It was nerve-wracking and I couldn't stand it.

"What?" I turned my head to look at him.

"Nothing." He turned his head turned quickly away from me. His hands were in his lap, folded tightly around a dripping wet notebook. Or maybe it was a journal. He glanced at me again, caught me staring at the journal. "It's ruined." His voice shook. It was almost like he'd lost his best friend. "I forgot I had it on me and now it's ruined." He squeezed his eyes shut, and I watched as a few tears trickled down his pale skin.

"It's just a book."

That was entirely the wrong thing to say, but I didn't realise it until I saw him tense up.

"It's not." He shook his head. "It's not just a book." He bent in on himself as if to protect the book.

"I write in it. It knows *everything*. And now it's ruined." He was crying for real now.

This situation made me extremely uncomfortable. So maybe he wasn't some lost boy who only needed a place to crash. I was pretty sure there was more to it than that. Much more. People didn't just start crying like that over a book, did they?

Maybe they did, and I was too emotionally stunted to know.

I stood up and headed into my room without a word to him. I knew I had a couple of those small sized notebooks somewhere that I hadn't used for school. I rummaged in the drawers of my desk and finally came up with a couple. I picked the nicest one, the one that had a leather-bound jacket and a string of leather to wrap around it. I had never intended to use it for school. I'd bought it just because it'd looked nice, but I had no use for it.

"Here." I held it out to him once I was back in the living room.

He lifted his head slowly, blinking the tears out of his eyes. "What's that?"

"You can have this if you want." I didn't know *why* I was giving him a brand new book, but he'd seemed absolutely heartbroken at his own being ruined, and that had torn at my own heartstrings.

His hand shook slightly as he reached out to take the book from me. He ran his fingers over it, feeling the leather and following the string around. He unwound it and opened the book, feeling the paper.

"Thank you." He gave me a small smile now, and that smile transformed his whole face. He wasn't adorable anymore—he was gorgeous.

"We can try to dry it." I nodded to the wet book still in his lap. "Maybe you can salvage it."

He shook his head, expression morphing into one of sadness again. "The ink's smudged. Can't read it."

I sat back down next to him. "Why are you so attached to a book?" I threw notebooks away all the time without a second thought.

"It keeps me sane," he whispered. "To write everything down, I mean. It's all I've got."

No friends. Only a journal. That was so sad.

I couldn't boast about being popular either, exactly. I had one friend—my *best* friend—and I was happy with that. It wasn't so long ago I didn't even have that, so I could sympathise with him. It wasn't fun not having anyone. Everyone needed *someone*.

"Do you have—?" I wasn't sure how to phrase it. I wished Silver was home so he could do all the talking for me. I wasn't good at this. "Do you have it tough? At home?"

He pursed his lips then shook his head. "Not really. Not anymore."

"Then why don't you want to go home?"

He stiffened again. "You want me to go home?"

"I want you to *want* to go home," I said. "No one should have to feel like they can't go home unless there's a reason for it."

He deflated next to me. "It's been a bad day. And they're all there, and they'll try to make me feel better —and I can't. I can't feel better about it no matter what they say. Eight years for making my life a living hell. What's the fairness in that?"

I had no idea what he was talking about, but I could guess one thing: it was bad.

Life a living hell, eight years… Eight years of what? Probation? Prison? Could be either. Most likely the latter, considering. But then again, what was so bad a person went to prison for it? I didn't even let my mind go there because there were endless possibilities.

"I like that they're all there, being all supportive and stuff, but today… I just can't today."

"Well, you can stay here tonight. But you'll have to share my bed. We don't have a guest room or anything." Why in the world was I offering to share a bed with him? I never shared my bed with anyone. I couldn't remember ever actually sleeping in the same bed as someone else. Maybe when I was young, when my sisters were still around.

He nodded jerkily. "You're very kind."

Not many people would use that word about me. I guess there was a first time for everything.

"Are you hungry?" I asked, for lack of anything else to say.

"Not really."

I wasn't either. "Tired?"

He nodded.

I pushed myself up, and he trailed silently after me into my bedroom. I went directly to my dresser, where I took out my pyjamas. "I'm just going to— um, the bathroom," I muttered, and then almost hightailed it out of my own room.

Being in the living room had been fine, but seeing him sink down on my bed, looking so sad and lost, had touched something in me. Something nothing else had ever touched, at least not for a great many years.

I took several deep breaths once I'd locked myself in the bathroom.

He was obviously depressed. He felt like he couldn't go home, even if he had a family there that he'd said he liked. He was lost, alone, dealing with something, something that must be really bad. And he had no friends to turn to. He needed a friend to turn to, for when he couldn't turn to his family.

I could be that friend.

I only had one friend, so I suppose I had room for one more.

CHAPTER 2

JOSH

I did my breathing exercises as I took in the room around me.

He had a desk where a laptop sat open, but it was turned off. There were several notebooks lying in a neat stack next to it, as well as a pencil case. He had books everywhere: on the desk, on the bookshelves, and on his nightstand.

Everything was neat though. Seemed he liked things to be in order. Even his bed was made.

Speaking of the bed… It wasn't the biggest. A three-quarter instead of a regular double. I guess it would be fine though. I wasn't exactly wide, and neither was he. *It's going to be okay.*

I was still sitting on the edge, unable to decide

what to do next, when he came back in. He was in pyjama trousers and a t-shirt, and he crossed his arms over his chest as his eyes fell on me. "Have you decided what side you want to sleep on?"

I frowned slightly. "Why don't you come sit down?" I patted the bed next to me.

He eyed me, seeming almost suspicious, but he did come over to take a seat. I turned to him, and his head tilted towards me. I took his face in. It was square, masculine, with pronounced cheekbones. His eyes were blue—azure maybe?—and his hair was black. He was handsome. Very handsome. This wouldn't be a chore at all.

"What?" His voice was harsh, impatient.

I better get to it.

I bent forward and pressed my lips to his in a soft kiss. He sat frozen for several long seconds, and I continued kissing him through them. His lips were soft. If only they'd start to reciprocate—

"What are you doing?"

He splayed his hands on my chest and pushed me away. He wasn't harsh in his movements, more gentle than anything, but it was still a push, a rejection, and my heart dropped to my stomach.

"You don't want to shag?" I cocked my head to the side, unsure and confused and starting to get really embarrassed.

"Wha—No!" He almost choked on the words. "What makes you think that?" He twitched uncomfortably.

"Everybody wants sex." I reached out with one hand, trying to put it high up on his thigh, but he slapped it away. I drew it back against my chest as if I'd been burned.

"I don't want that. I didn't ask you here for that." He was spluttering. Clearly sex hadn't even been on his mind. "That's wrong in so many ways. I'm pretty sure it's illegal."

"Like people care." I inched my other hand back to his thigh, hoping he was more open to it now that his mind had been turned to sex. "Nobody says no to sex when it's offered on a silver platter. Are you straight?"

"No." He shook his head jerkily.

"So you are gay?" Maybe it was just me he didn't want to have sex with. I couldn't blame him.

"No. I'm not anything," he snapped. His hand locked around my wrist before I could inch away from him, and pain shot up my arm from the firm grip. I jerked back with a pained grimace. "What's wrong with you? Have you sprained your arm or something?"

He pulled my sleeve up without permission to look at my arm. Except it wasn't my arm meeting him, but tightly wrapped gauze. Gauze that was wet and had patches of red dotted all over it.

He blinked a couple of times, taking it in. "This should be changed."

He touched one of the red spots, and I flinched back, further away from him. He stared up at me then resolutely unwound the gauze.

"No, don't—" I protested, but it was too late. The bottom half of my forearm was already bared to view.

I heard him draw in a shaky breath at the sight that met him. I didn't even have to look down. I knew what was there. Scars upon scars, cuts upon cuts, and blood. Coagulated blood and fresh blood. I'd cut deep. Many of the cuts hadn't had the chance to clot yet.

"Is this why you can't go home?" He stared. His hand held mine, and it was warm and big and firm, but his eyes stared at my mutilated skin. It made me antsy.

"Part of it, I guess." My voice had dropped to a whisper. "I have my reasons for doing this. I'm not proud of it, but I can't stop." I pulled my arm out of his grip and did a poor job at rewrapping the wet and bloody gauze.

He still stared at my arm.

"I didn't mean to offend you," I continued when he didn't say anything. "I'm used to people wanting to shag, you know? People don't help me without wanting something in return, and all I can give is sex. That's all I know." All I'd ever known.

"I don't want that." He said it firmly too, driving the words in deep.

"I'm sorry for thinking you did." I bowed my head, mortified and embarrassed and so incredibly sad. He was a handsome bloke. He'd been nice to me, he'd offered to let me stay, but he didn't want more than that. He didn't want me.

"Can I change your gauze?" He was *still* staring at my arm.

"Okay." I didn't want him to see my arms in full, but the gauze was uncomfortable. He offered to help me, and I would take whatever he had to give.

I followed him into the bathroom, where I sank down on the edge of the tub. I'd hung my wet clothes up to dry on the clothing lines above it and water dripped from them.

He rummaged around in a drawer and in the cabinets. He came up with clean gauze, a washcloth he wetted under the tap, and antibacterial.

I unwound the old gauze, just to have something to do. Both arms were bared to him now. The horror of what I'd done to myself. I was ashamed he'd seen it in the first place. If he hadn't forced the issue, I would've gone to sleep with the wet gauze and dealt with it being uncomfortable. But when he offered help... I couldn't *not* take it.

"Does blood bother you?" I glanced up, curious.

"No." He shook his head for emphasis as he crouched down in front of me. "Doesn't bother me at all. What does is that you do this to yourself. They'll never go away, the scars."

"I know." I stared down at my own arms. I turned them over, showing off the undersides. They looked even worse. The thin skin over both my wrists was even more a mess of criss-crossed scars than the rest. I could see his eyes trained on the deep scars there. "That's how I tried to kill myself."

I hadn't meant for that to slip out. I didn't want him to think I was mental, though he probably thought that anyway. I didn't want to confirm it, but my mouth had decided to prove just what an unstable person I was without my consent.

I could feel my face burn in shame.

He didn't say anything, just started to clean me up.

"Thank you," I said after a while.

"For what?" He dabbed antibacterial on the washcloth, and I hissed as he ran it over my fresh cuts.

"For being so nice. No one has ever been this kind to me before. Not when they don't expect anything. Which you don't. Not even then, really."

"No, I don't."

There it was again, the confirmation that he didn't find me attractive.

"Why not? Why don't you want it? Are you in a relationship?" I couldn't help but press the issue. If he was in a relationship, I could understand why he would reject me. No one liked a cheater.

"No, I'm not." He wrapped new, clean gauze around my right forearm. "I just... I just don't want it, is all." He started in on my left arm, and I hissed again once the antibacterial came into contact with fresh cuts.

"You've done this a lot? You seem very good at it." His fingers were long and slender, and they patched me up with an ease I never showed when I did this myself.

He glanced up at me. Our eyes met and held for a second. "What'd you mean?"

"This." I lifted my right arm up. "You seem really good at patching people up. So have you done it a lot?"

"No." A brief shake of the head. "I'm starting medical school. I want to be a surgeon."

Oh, wow. I didn't even know what to say to that.

"Medical school, huh? You must be real smart." *So lame.* That was the lamest thing I'd said until now. I should've just kept my mouth shut.

"I do the best I can. It's what I want to do."

"You're lucky then. I don't know what I want to do. I'm just a big mess."

"You'll figure it out."

"I want to help people. People who struggle. People who've been through what I have. But I'm a complete mess myself, so how can I even begin to help someone else?" My voice had a bitter tone to it now. Not knowing what I wanted to do with my life was galling. Sometimes I was resentful that I even had a life.

"Going to uni is always a good start," he commented as he wrapped gauze around my left arm as well.

I snorted. "And study what? Psychology? When I don't even understand my own? That wouldn't go over well. Besides, I've failed my A-levels."

Once he finished of the gauze, he leant back so he could look up at me properly.

My eyes zeroed in on his lips, but I knew he would just push me away again if I tried to kiss him. I wasn't setting myself up for another bout of rejection. I wasn't sure I could take that. Not today.

"Better?" he asked.

"Yeah." I bobbed my head. I felt over the new gauze. Dry and soft and clean.

"Now can we go to sleep?" He pushed himself up on his feet and put away everything he'd used. He threw the old gauze in the rubbish and headed out the door.

That had me moving. I followed close to him, back into his bedroom again.

"So what side do you want to sleep on?" He wasn't looking at me when he asked.

I looked towards the bed. From the way it was positioned against the wall, as well as the books and mobile phone on the nightstand, I took a guess that he slept close to it.

I got on the bed and scooted over to lie close to the wall. I slipped under the duvet, thankful that he had two in his bed. I didn't think he'd want to be any closer to me than he had to be.

I could tell he was nervous as he slid in beside me. "You never shared a bed with anyone?" I couldn't help but ask because it was so very obvious from the way he was acting.

He shook his head. "No."

"Why do you have two duvets then, if you always sleep alone?"

He shrugged awkwardly. "I usually use both. I get cold at night."

That was a logical explanation. "Don't worry. I won't try anything. You made yourself clear."

He licked his lips nervously. "Good." He reached over the bedside table to turn off the lamp.

It plummeted me into total darkness at first, but once my eyes adjusted, it wasn't all that dark. I could still see him next to me though his features weren't that clear to me anymore. I didn't think he would appreciate me looking at him though, so I kept my eyes trained on the ceiling.

That's when I realised something.

Something important.

"I don't know your name."

"Damian," he answered shortly.

Damian. "That's a nice name. I'm Josh."

His head turned to me, and I could see his frown. I was pretty sure he was trying to decide if I was mad or not. The first wouldn't be far from the truth, actually.

"I don't know how to repay you for this."

"You don't have to repay me. I didn't ask you here to get anything in return."

"But that book you gave me, that seemed expensive. I'll pay you back for that one, at least."

"No, really, it's okay. Don't. I wasn't going to use it anyway."

I turned over on my side and curled up. "You're really kind."

"No more than anyone else." His head was still tilted towards me. Our eyes met and held.

"More than anyone I've ever met."

He frowned again. "Then you can't have met many decent people."

"Maybe not," I agreed. My chest squeezed tight at the thought though. It squeezed and it squeezed until I felt like I was going to explode. I wasn't sure if I wanted to cry or rage—maybe both at the same time.

"I couldn't leave you out there," he said, breaking into my thoughts. "If you feel you can't go home, you can always come here. I know what it's like to feel that way." His voice had dropped to a whisper on the last sentence.

"Did you have it tough when you lived at home?" My thoughts were easily diverted, and that's exactly what his words had done: diverted my thoughts from my own trauma to his.

"I used to. Way back. Not so much now. I love my uncle and aunt and my cousins. But it's difficult."

"What's difficult?" I wasn't sure why, but it made me feel a tiny bit better to know that I wasn't the only one with a messed up life.

"I don't know. Everything. Nothing. It shouldn't be difficult because all they've done is be there for me, but it is. And it's all on me, I know, but I guess that's just who I am." He let out a deep breath then turned his head away from me. Maybe he was embarrassed.

"I think you're wonderful," was all I could come up with. It was the truth though. No one had done for me what he had, and for that I would be eternally grateful.

He chuckled but didn't say anything.

"I'll go home tomorrow. I just needed to get away for a while. Maybe tomorrow it'll be better."

"What'll be better?"

"Everything. I don't know." Nothing would be, I knew, but I had to go home. My mum must be beside herself, for sure. So must the rest of them, for that matter. I hadn't brought my mobile with me when I left, only my journal, so they wouldn't be able to get a hold of me.

Maybe it was shitty of me to stay away for the night without letting them know, but I needed space.

"A little bit better, at least." Saying that would perhaps make everything feel better.

I reached out tentatively, under the duvets, and fumbled for his hand. When I found it, I squeezed it, trying to pour all my gratitude into it. Hoping to show him just how much it meant to me.

He didn't squeeze my hand in return, which saddened me, but he didn't move his hand away either.

I guess I could count that as a win.

CHAPTER 3

DAMIAN

I couldn't sleep.

Josh lay beside me. We weren't touching, but he wasn't far from me either. I could feel his warmth, and his breathing was slow and even. He was fast asleep.

I turned on my side. Slowly, so I wouldn't jolt the bed and wake him up. He was lying on his stomach, his head facing me and with his arm curled under his cheek.

I reached my hand out to run my index finger over his bandaged forearm. The sight of those arms, sans the gauze, was branded into my brain. I couldn't believe that people would do that to themselves. That they'd hurt themselves so bad, in such a way that they would always bear the scars afterwards. Josh would never be rid of them—they'd always be there, on his skin, always a reminder.

Josh's face was relaxed. He looked adorable, and I ran my hand up his cheek. His skin there was soft, so different from his arms.

I moved my hand around to his neck, to play with the soft hair at his nape.

I couldn't seem to get enough of looking at him. Even if the curtains were closed, there was still enough light in the room from the summer night outside to see him. Not quite clear, but not far from it.

I've only known him for a few hours and already I can't get enough of him.

What was wrong with me?

This was unlike me. I didn't get attached to people. Yet Josh had managed to get under my skin. He'd kissed me. I'd never reacted to anyone before—but I had to him. What was so special about him?

I pulled my hand back. I didn't want to wake him, not when he was sleeping so soundly. I suspected he didn't always, not with all those scars on his arms. Something made him do that to himself and I suspected it mostly happened at night. Night was the loneliest time of the day, after all.

I inched out of bed then tip-toed out of the room and into the bathroom.

I turned the tap on and splashed some water on

my face. When I looked up into the mirror, I met my own eyes; I couldn't help but ask myself what I was doing. I wasn't fit to get close to anyone, yet that was exactly what I felt was happening. What was more, he seemed to be more unfit for it than I was.

A knock on the door drew my focus, and I grabbed a towel to dry my face before answering it.

Silver pushed it open before I could say anything though, and he shut if softly behind him before walking over to sit on the edge of the tub, just like Josh had done earlier.

"You all right?" he asked, his expression serious. His grey eyes were intense as they took me in.

"Yeah." I eyed him in return, not sure what he was getting at.

"You're having a sleep-over." That sentence sounded like a mix between a statement and a question.

"I guess." Sleep-over? That sounded so juvenile. It wasn't like we were doing anything other than sleeping though. *Except that kiss.* But I'd broken that off before he could've taken it any further. "It's not what you think. He doesn't have anywhere else to go." I wiped the towel over my face again, mostly just to have something to do besides fidget under Silver's stare.

Silver raised a black eyebrow. "You brought home a homeless bloke?"

"He's not homeless." I glared at him. "He just can't go home right now." I wasn't sure why I was defending Josh so hotly, but Silver had sounded scandalous at the thought of him being homeless and now in our home.

"Okay." Silver nodded, slow and thoughtful, allowing me to calm down. "I thought you were asexual."

I put the towel down on the sink and scratched awkwardly over my chest. "I am. Was. I don't know." I shook my head to get rid of all my fluttering thoughts. It didn't help. "I don't know what this is." All I knew was I couldn't get enough of looking at him; I'd liked his kiss even if I'd pushed him away, and his hand squeezing mine underneath the duvets had been *good*.

"How long have you known him?"

"Couple of hours."

"What? *Hours?*" Silver was incredulous now. I couldn't blame him. "When you do get out there, you really do it properly, don't you?" He whistled.

I flushed in embarrassment and grabbed onto the sink for support. "I haven't done anything. I just offered him a place to stay tonight. He was sad and alone and soaked through."

"So you haven't done it?"

I glanced at him in confusion. His face was split into a grin, and I realised in an instant what he was talking about. "No!" My face heated up further.

"So what then? You've found yourself another asexual?" Silver was getting more and more confused. As was to be expected, considering just how confused *I* was by it all.

"No." I turned around and sunk to the floor, resting my back against the cabinets under the sink. "He offered, but I declined."

Silver's eyebrows inched up his forehead again. "You declined sex? Who declines sex?" I glowered at him, but it didn't shut him up. "I thought you'd get over the no-sex thing once you met someone. I though the asexual thing was just a joke. I'm sorry." He was being sincere now.

"What are you sorry for?"

"For not taking you seriously, I guess. I mean, I know you haven't been interested in these kinds of things before, but I always figured it would change once you met someone. It was shitty of me to assume that. You know your body, your sexuality, better than anyone."

"No, not really," I cut him off before he could continue. "I thought I did, but I—I don't." He didn't have to apologise. I didn't understand myself, so how could he?

Not even my uncle and aunt understood me, though they did care for me. My cousins, they were just kids. My aunt's sister thought I was a freak, though she'd always used to tell me so in an affectionate voice. They all cared, but they didn't understand me. I was too different from everyone I knew, even my best friend.

Silver leant back slightly and crossed his arms over his chest. His face and eyes were dead serious as they looked down on me. "I couldn't help but notice the bloody gauze in the rubbish bin. You hurt yourself?"

I shook my head mutely.

"Has he?"

I wasn't sure if I could tell him. I didn't know what the proper way here was. I'd only had one friend in my entire life, and he was sitting in front of me. I wasn't sure if Josh's cutting was a secret or not.

But Silver had an attention for detail—he had to, being a tattoo artist.

"Self-harm," I muttered.

"Oh." Silver's expression didn't change, though his eyes got thoughtful. "Do you think it's wise to get involved with someone so messed up? Self-harm…

There's got to be some heavy underlying issues there, mate."

"But haven't I got that too?" I propped my elbows on my knees and buried my hands in my thick hair. "I haven't got the amount of scars that he has, but mine's a heck of a lot bigger than any of the ones he had."

Silver's serious expression softened. "Maybe two scarred souls can make each other whole."

"That was deep," I said drily. "And oddly poetic."

Silver grinned. "So how is it that my asexual best mate finds himself a boyfriend before I do?"

"He's not my boyfriend." Not even close. He wasn't even my friend—not yet anyway. Silver was right, anyway: Josh did have a lot of issues. Lots more than the cutting, for sure.

"He's sharing your *bed*," Silver pointed out. "You don't have the biggest bed, you know, and you don't even seem to mind that he's there."

Boyfriend. That was a relationship. With another human being.

Was that what I wanted?

It was too early to say, obviously, but I couldn't help but think I might. I'd never had a reaction to anyone the way I reacted to Josh. In just a few hours, he'd turned my life completely up-side-down.

"I'm going back to bed." I pushed myself up.

"Let me know when you know." Silver was back to grinning widely.

I smiled slightly as I headed over to the door.

The smile died once I entered my bedroom and found Josh thrashing on the bed.

I hurried over to the side of the bed. "Josh?" I put my knees on the bed, wondering what to do. He was having a nightmare, that much was obvious, but what should I do about it? What would be the best thing to do? "Josh?"

I didn't want to grab him, as I knew from experience that that could make whatever nightmare he was having worse. But I also didn't want him to do something that would hurt his already injured and bandaged arms any further. What if he started bleeding again?

Josh's eyes opened, and he gasped as he scrambled away from me. His eyes were wild with fear.

"It's me. Damian." I held my hands out, palms towards him, to show that I wasn't going to hurt him.

He blinked. The fear from the nightmare disappeared gradually as he finally recognised me. He didn't move from his position against the wall though, but his left hand inched over to scratch at the gauze on his right.

"Don't do that." I scooted over to him and gently

wrapped my hands around his arms, pulling them apart. "Don't hurt yourself."

"It's nothing compared to what hurts in *here*." He pulled one arm free and splayed his fingers over his chest, over his heart. "It hurts *so* much."

"I know." I did know how much pain he could feel on the inside could, but I wasn't going to stand by and watch him cause harm to his outside. Not when he was here with me.

He bent his head and then gently prodded his other arm out of my grip too. He slowly lay back down on the bed, curling up on himself.

I lay back down too, on my back. It would be better to stare at the ceiling for now instead of at him.

"I hate dreaming about him," he whispered. "He hasn't done anything to me in so long, but I still dream about all the horrible things he used to do."

My chest squeezed. I didn't know who he was talking about, but it was obvious from the anguish in his voice, not to mention the nightmare itself and the reaction it had provoked, that it couldn't be anything good.

I supposed it wasn't possible to forget the bad things that happened. After all, didn't people tend to remember the bad memories rather than the good ones? I was certainly fixated on the bad, no matter how many years ago it was now.

I tilted my head to the side. Josh was lying with his back to me, and he was so tense he quivered.

I didn't think about my decision. I just rolled over and put my arm over his middle, squeezing him tight for a few moments before I settled down close to him. "Okay?"

"More than okay," he whispered in a choked voice. "It's perfect."

He gradually relaxed against me. I wasn't sure if he was asleep or not, but his breathing had evened out and he seemed to be content.

I was glad, because the nightmare he'd had, that had been terrible. Whoever it was he'd been dreaming about, it was bad.

My body had reacted to him earlier, to his brief kiss. I hadn't given in though, and I wasn't about to. Both because I didn't want to and because I was certain he needed to see that not everyone was inter-ested in sex. His words proved that that was his train of thought. As far as I could tell, his whole life had been about sex—whilst mine had never been.

I wasn't sure if it ever would.

But the kiss had been good.

CHAPTER 4

JOSH

I couldn't sleep. Damian had fallen asleep a while ago and rolled over onto his other side. I sat up in bed and watched him for a moment in the darkened room.

His T-shirt stretched over his back. His arms were toned—not muscular, per se, but he was fit. The duvet covered him from the middle of the back and down, so I couldn't see what he looked like further down. Not that I needed to know what hid beneath the duvet, not really. There was more than enough to look at already.

He was handsome. So very handsome.

I scooted down so I could get off the bed without having to crawl over him. He didn't react as I pushed myself up on my feet and tip-toed out of the room.

I didn't know why I'd left the room at all, because it wasn't like there was much else I could do in the flat. I couldn't leave, not while wearing his clothes and with mine drying, but at least I wouldn't be tossing and turning and risk waking him up.

The flat was dark, so his flatmate must be asleep as well.

If he was even at home. I hadn't seen anything of him earlier, after all.

I sat down on the sofa. It was soft, comfortable.

My fingers itched. For a razor, for a pen, for something to do. I wasn't good by myself. I always ended up with a razor, though sometimes pen and paper could help just as much as the razor.

I did have the journal Damian had given me. It was lying there, on the table.

But I didn't have a pen.

I didn't have a razor either.

My nightmare had left me on edge. I'd been able to relax when he'd been lying close to me, with his arm wrapped around me, but once he rolled away I was back to being my usual jumpy, nervous, uncomfortable self.

I could never feel at peace, and it was exhausting.

I jumped in my seat when a door at my side opened. I didn't know what I'd been expecting, considering the two options I had, but I somehow hadn't expected Damian's flatmate to emerge.

He caught sight of me and stopped next to the sofa. "Hey."

"H-hey." I was still rattled. It was the middle of the night; I hadn't seen it coming.

"What are you doing?"

"Can't sleep." I wrapped my arms around my middle and bent over slightly. "You?"

"Can't sleep either." He watched me calmly. "D out cold?" He motioned his head in the direction of Damian's door.

"Yeah." I nodded. "Why can't you sleep?"

"Bad dreams." He said it matter-of-factly, which told me it was a usual occurrence. "What about you?"

I had to smile slightly at that. "Bad dreams."

He chuckled. "Those are the worst, aren't they?"

"Y-yeah." I'd be glad if I could have the regular nightmares normal people had, random and not all long-ago memories. But all I dreamt about was *him*. I hated dreaming about him.

"I was just getting myself a glass of water." He pointed at the kitchen. "Can I get you anything?"

I started shaking my head, then reconsidered. "Do you have a pen? And paper to write on?"

He blinked, surprised. "Yeah, sure." He went

back into his bedroom and came out with a notebook and pen, which he put down on the table in front of me. "Anything else?"

"No, thanks. This is fine." I held the pen in my hand, clenching my fist around it.

"I'll get my water then." He disappeared into the kitchen. I heard a cupboard open and the sink running then he walked back past me. "Goodnight."

"Goodnight." I watched his broad back disappear into his room before I returned my focus to the notebook as the door closed.

I didn't know what to write.

All I knew was that I wanted to write something, wanted to get my thoughts and my feelings down on this paper.

"Joshua!"

Grandma descended on me the moment I stepped through the doors. Her hands, seemingly so frail and wrinkled, had a surprising strength to them as they gripped my face. She turned my head to each side, taking me in, checking for—I don't even know what she was checking for.

"Morning."

Her eyes were a mix of worry and anger and

relief. "We've been worried sick. You left yesterday without a word, and we haven't been able to get a hold of you. Why would you leave your mobile? Why wouldn't you let us know where you were? Joshua." My name came out on a relieved sigh, and then she hugged me.

"I'm okay." I patted her back awkwardly.

I wasn't used to hugs.

She hadn't visited very often until two years ago, and it wasn't like I'd been smothered by my mother before then either.

In fact, the first hug I could remember from my mum was at the hospital that time.

"Where have you been? Your mum said you don't know anybody. Have you been outside all night?" She pulled back, eyes taking me in again, now from head to toe and back up.

"I met someone," I hurried to explain because I didn't want her thinking I'd rather be out on the streets than here at home. Though it was the truth, so I wasn't being entirely truthful now.

Still, a white lie to keep her from worrying more couldn't hurt, right?

Her eyebrows drew together in a frown. "Joshua—"

"It's okay." I cut her off before she could continue.

I knew what she was thinking: that I'd hooked up with someone.

I used to do that.

I wasn't doing it anymore.

I hadn't been out for that purpose in months now, and after last night... I wasn't sure I wanted to anymore. "It's not like that."

It should worry me, or weird me out, that my grandma knew so much about my sex life, but they all knew the deep, dark secret I'd kept for years now. And after that, nothing was too private not to be shared.

"I'm going to call your mum." Grandma stepped back, out of my personal space. "She didn't want to go in to work this morning, but I told her I'd stay here and wait for you."

I nodded, not sure what else to say.

Once she left me, I headed into my bedroom.

My mobile was on my desk and I picked it up. There was nothing new on it besides the missed calls from my entire family yesterday.

No new texts though or anything.

But then it hadn't been that long since I left, so maybe Damian hadn't had time to read the letter I wrote. Or see the number I'd scribbled at the end of it.

I wasn't at all confident that he would be in

contact. He didn't seem like the kind of person to take the initiative.

I had only asked for friendship though.

Friendship was good, safe.

He couldn't reject friendship, could he?

Sex was all right. It had been a part of my life for so long. But he'd rejected me on that—and I'd been *grateful* for a moment there. Grateful that I didn't have to perform for him, no matter how much I'd actually wanted to when I'd kissed him.

Now I wasn't so sure what I felt.

My mind was a right mess, and I didn't know what to do about it.

But that wasn't anything out of the ordinary.

I SUNK DOWN HEAVILY in my usual space in Vincent's office. He sat opposite me, his dark eyes resting on me.

I had my new journal clutched to my chest. I hadn't written in it yet, but I wanted it with me.

My mind was still in turmoil, and I rocked back and forth for a bit. I knew Vincent was watching me, taking me and my odd behaviour in, but I couldn't help it.

"I met someone last night," I started in a low

voice. "He was... very handsome. I offered myself to him, and I think he wanted me, but then he just—He said no."

I still had difficulty wrapping my head around it. "I threw myself at him and he said no."

Vincent folded his hands in his lap. "How'd that make you feel?"

"I don't know." It felt like my brain was walking in circles. "I have no idea how that made me feel. I guess, rejected. I mean, who says *no* to sex?" I was shaking my head to myself. "I feel really weird. I can't even explain it."

"What kind of weird?" Vincent was as calm as ever.

"I don't know." I clutched my journal tighter. "All my life's been about sex. It's all I know. If I can't do that, then what do I have?"

"Who says you can't have sex?"

"N-no one." I blinked. "But he said no. In my experience, people don't do that."

Vincent watched me in silence for a few moments. "You ended our last session two days ago by saying you finally felt free. Tell me about that."

I frowned in thought. "Well, he's getting locked away, no question about that. No matter what happens, the years, he'll be incarcerated, and I won't have to be afraid anymore." I bent in on myself. "I've been afraid for so long, and after yesterday, I don't have to be anymore. He's off the streets now. No bail for him. Just prison. And I hope he rots in there." I really did. I didn't want him to ever get out again.

"How many years did he get?"

"Eight," I whispered, terror coursing through me for a moment. Eight years and he'd be back out. Back out where I could meet him. Where he could find me. "Eight years."

"How does that make you feel?"

"At first I was relieved because that meant that I would be free for the next eight years. But now it terrifies me because eight years isn't that long, and then he'll be back out again where he can seek me out and hurt me." My breath hitched involuntarily. "He's made my life a living hell, and he only got *eight* years. It's not fair!" The tears were running again, like they'd done last night once the numbness had worn off.

I'd had the same thought then as I was having now. "I don't know what to do, Vincent. Some days are bearable, but most days I just wish I'd pressed the razor a little bit deeper and taken just a few more pills."

I had been so *close* only to wake up in the hospital and be told I'd been lucky, that I'd be all right. I hadn't felt lucky. I'd felt anything but. Even with the truth finally out, with my mum actually believing me, I hadn't felt any kind of fortune at the situation.

"Have you taken your medication today, Josh?"

I cast around for a memory of taking them, but I couldn't find any.

Not from today.

Not from yesterday either.

"N-no." I didn't like being dependant on pills, but I didn't like feeling how I did now either. At least with the pills, I was a little calmer, a little more balanced, and a little less emotionally unstable.

"Taking your medication is your job now, Josh. When you were hospitalised, you were given your dosage everyday so you wouldn't forget, but now that you're home it's up to you."

"I know. I know that." I ran a hand through my hair. "It's just been a difficult few days."

"All the more reason to take them."

I knew he was right. He was always right.

And I was always a mess.

I WALKED out of therapy not feeling any better than I had going in. I didn't know what to do with myself now that I was done either. Going back home meant being surrounded by everyone, which could be nice, but it could also lead to a disaster because my cousins were a bit too much at times.

I didn't have anyone else though, did I?

Maybe I did.

He still hadn't texted me, but he'd mentioned something about work before I'd left his flat that morning. I'd asked him where he worked, and he'd told me Harriet's Café in Soho. There couldn't be that many cafés by that name in Soho, could there?

I cast around for reasons to do one or the other, but I couldn't come up with any, neither pros nor cons.

If I turned right, the way led towards home, but if I turned left, further into the city.

I took the left turn.

DAMIAN

I know I told you thank you for everything, but I want you to know just how thankful I am. That you talked to me, that you let me into your home—that means more to me than I can ever express in words. I've never been good with words, not vocal ones anyway. I do much better in writing.

So thank you. So much.

You were kind to me without expecting anything in return, which is completely unlike how I've always known people to be. You showed me otherwise, so thank you for that.

Tonight was special. It was nice and unlike any other night I've ever experienced. I don't want to go back to not experiencing this again. I want to get to know you—

and I hope you want to get to know me too. It felt like you did—when I wasn't hitting on you, anyway.

You seem like a good bloke. I wish we could be friends. I need some of those because I don't actually have anyone.

That sounded pathetic, didn't it? Still, it's true. I'm being honest. I'm trying my best to always be honest. They tell me it's good for me and I have to agree. Keeping secrets was what led me to being the mess that I am today, after all.

I'm sorry. This isn't a very good inquiry for friendship.

But then again, you saw my arms. You cleaned me up. You didn't judge. You didn't even ask or tell me I couldn't keep doing this to myself.

I know what I do to myself is wrong, that it's not healthy, but having people constantly be on me about it is counter-productive.

You weren't though, and I'm so grateful.

So I hope we can be friends.

I would like that very much.

I hope you do too.

—JOSH

CHAPTER 5

DAMIAN

I was in the kitchen, washing dishes, when Leslie stuck his head in the doorway. I didn't react, expecting him to be looking for Harriet.

"Hey, Damian, there's someone here asking for you. Or at least I think it was you." Leslie had a northern accent, which I sometimes found difficult to understand when I wasn't paying attention, but that sentence wasn't hard at all. It was very clear.

"For me?" I frowned as I snapped off the rubber gloves. He bobbed his head. "What do you mean you think it's me?" I wiped my hands at my apron. They were all clammy from the gloves.

"He started asking, getting half your name out, then I think he saw something, and now he's not saying anything at all."

What?

I went to the front, confused as to what was going on. It couldn't be me. Who would be here asking for me?

But it was.

It was Josh.

"Josh?"

He was staring out the window, face expression-less, with a far-away look in his eyes. It seemed to be a lot more than him just being deep in thought, and it scared me.

"Josh?"

I walked to his side, and when he still didn't react, I snapped my fingers in front of his eyes.

He blinked and flinched away. Then his wide eyes settled on me, and recognition flashed in them.

I turned to Leslie, who was at the counter. "Okay if I take a second break?"

He nodded again, watching us both curiously.

I put my arm around Josh's shoulders and led him to the back, to the room we used for changing and breaks.

I pushed him down on the sofa then sat down next to him. "What are you doing here?"

"I wanted to see you. You didn't text me."

"I've been at work." I reminded him gently.

No matter how gentle my tone was though, he

seemed to take it the wrong way. "I'm sorry. I shouldn't have come here."

"It's okay," I assured him. "I don't mind. I was just wondering."

He seemed so frail where he sat, curled in on himself.

I put my hand on his shoulder blade and rubbed softly, hoping it would calm him down and reassure him that I really was fine with him being here.

"What was that out there? You were completely checked out."

His tongue flicked out to wet his lip. "I thought I saw him. I know, rationally, that it couldn't *be* him because he's in prison—but that man looked so much like him."

I didn't know what to say. I still didn't know who *he* was, and I didn't know what he'd done to cause Josh to be so afraid of him. So I settled on just rubbing his back in what I hoped were soothing circles. I'd never done this before, never tried to make someone else feel better.

I don't think I was any good at it because he didn't seem to be feeling better.

"You said you worked here, so I just wanted to stop by." He shrugged awkwardly.

"That's nice," was all I could think to say in return. It was nice that he wanted to see me again, but at the same time it was perhaps a little disturbing. Something was clearly wrong with him, and he'd come to *me*.

But he had said he didn't have any friends.

Maybe he was just lonely?

I could understand that, though I mostly preferred being on my own.

And that letter he'd written me... Well, if that didn't tell me he was lonely, then nothing could.

"Do you want to do something later, once I'm off work?" I found myself asking.

That simple question made him perk up. "You want that?"

I nodded. "Sure." How could such a simple question turn his mood around from depressed to hopeful? Was he that deprived from human companionship?

"What do you want to do?" He straightened up a bit, and his arms, which had been kept tight to his chest, finally fell to his lap. He had the journal I'd given him clutched in-between them.

I had no idea what I wanted to do.

What did people do when they spent time together? "How about going to the cinema?"

He nodded quickly. "I can pay for us."

"You don't have to do that."

"I want to. Please. Let me do something for you.

Just this small thing." His gaze was begging me, and I couldn't help but relent to it. I didn't want to say so out loud though, so I only nodded.

His reaction stunned me, because I received a smile in return. A smile so wide it showed teeth, and all I'd ever seen from him last night and this morning was a small one that barely turned the edges of his lips upwards.

The door opened, bringing my attention away from that smile. I wasn't sure if I was relieved or not to see Harriet standing there.

"Leslie said you took another break. Are you all right?"

Harriet owned the café, and she was the most wonderful boss one could ever wish to have. She was in her early thirties, with bright, auburn hair and green eyes. *Kind of the same colour as Josh's, only a little lighter.* She was strict about her business, but fair about her employees. If something happened, she worried.

"I'm fine." I glanced at Josh to find that the smile was gone, replaced by a frown as he watched Harriet. "I should get back to work."

Harriet glanced between us. "It's okay if you want to take a longer break. It's calm out there now that the lunch rush is over. Les and I are fine on our own."

I sank back down.

Harriet smiled at me. "I didn't mean to interrupt. Les just said you went back here, so I was worried."

"That's okay."

She shut the door softly behind her, leaving me once again alone with Josh. He was still frowning, and I found myself watching him silently.

He blushed once he realised I was looking at him. "What?"

"Nothing." I guess I was blushing a bit myself. I liked looking at him, even when he was frowning, and it was confusing. I'd never liked to look at anyone before now. In fact, I preferred to keep from looking too long at anyone *ever*.

"When do you get off work?"

"Couple of hours."

"Can I stay here? Wait for you?"

I finally dared to turn back to look at him.

He looked back at me hopefully.

"Still don't want to go home?"

He shook his head once.

"I guess you can. I'm sure Harriet won't mind."

"I can buy something, if that makes her happier," he offered.

"Whatever you want to do." I smiled slightly then stood up again. "I really should get back to work. Sure you want to stay here and wait for me?"

He nodded. "Just one thing. Do you have a pen?"

I looked down at my apron just to double-check, as I knew I always had pens there. I handed one to him. "You okay?"

"Yeah. Thanks." Another smile.

I didn't have any more excuses to stay, so I turned and went back out into the café. Part of me wasn't at all sure what I was getting myself into, while the other... The other prayed for the next two hours to go by quickly.

WE DECIDED ON A COMEDY. Comedies were light and hopefully wouldn't include some sappy romance that would make me squirm in my seat.

Besides, he needed some comedy in his life.

So did I for that matter.

He'd bought a small popcorn—salted, because sweetened was utterly disgusting. I wasn't sure if he liked it or not, but when I'd mentioned it, he'd happily ordered salted.

"It's been a while since I've been to the cinema." He glanced around the big room. There weren't that many people, since the film had been out for a while and those that were there were all sitting further down from us.

I was grateful I didn't have anyone behind me. Having someone behind me, even if they weren't directly, made me twitchy and nervous.

"You want some?" He held the popcorn out to me.

I looked down at it, originally intending not to as I hadn't bought my own, but he seemed to be in such a good mood, and I didn't want to dampen it. So I took a handful.

He smiled and turned back to the screen to watch the previews.

I couldn't get my mind to focus on them. Instead, all I could think about was him.

Was this just two mates hanging out? Or was this a date? Silver would call it a date, for sure, but I'd never been on one before. I didn't know if I even wanted to be on one.

The film started on the screen. I was looking that way, but I didn't see what was going on there. I was very much aware of Josh next to me, of his shoulder almost brushing up against mine.

So if this was a date... What was to be expected?

I should've asked Silver. But I hadn't known this morning I would find myself in a cinema with Josh. I'd only met him the day before, after all. I'd never anticipated actually developing any kind of feelings for him. How could that even be possible when we'd just met? There should be some kind of rule against that.

I jumped three feet in the air when his hand slid over to tentatively grab mine. I held my breath as he hesitated for a long moment then entwined our fingers when I didn't make a move to remove my hand.

His hand was soft and dry, whereas I was pretty sure my own was sweating by now. My heart beat double. It felt almost like it was about to beat out of my ribcage. I was suddenly desperate to actually watch the film, but I could feel him staring at me.

"What?" My voice was hoarse, and I managed to turn my head around to meet those green eyes.

"I'm sorry." He turned his head back around so quickly I was afraid he'd get whiplash.

"Why are you always apologising? You don't have to do that."

"What else can I say?" he replied in a murmur. "I know I'm intense. I know my mood swings are exhausting to other people. I'm a handful and I *know* it."

What?

How did we go from me asking why he was looking at me to him degrading himself? "You could just answer my question."

He drew his bottom lip in-between his teeth. "I like looking at you. You're... appealing."

Appealing? "Okay. Thanks. I guess."

His head turned back to me, and his eyes were big and wet. I felt caught in a cross-fire. Had I said something wrong? I didn't... think so. I cast around for anything, but as socially awkward as I was, I wasn't sure I could recognise it if it hit me in the face.

"D-do you?" His voice was shaking.

"Do I what?"

"Like me?"

That was it? "Yeah." It came out on a low breath, but his brightening expression told me he heard me loud and clear.

He smiled sheepishly. "Can I—Can I just—?" He didn't finish the question, but instead leaned in to kiss me.

His lips were soft and warm, and this was a lot more of a kiss than last night had been. It was my second kiss, period. When he'd kissed me last night, that had been my first.

I'd never kissed a person before, and now I'd kissed him twice.

Or did last night count, as I hadn't reciprocated? Since I'd pushed him away?

I'd never given kissing any thought. I hadn't understood what people liked about it so much.

Now I knew.

Feeling someone else's lips against my own... I didn't like being close to people, but being so close and intimate with Josh? It wasn't like anything I'd ever felt before.

His tongue ran over my lips now, and I tried my best to reciprocate it. It was a rather clumsy attempt, but it *was* my first reciprocated kiss, so I reckoned it would have to do.

Josh was a good kisser, and he was much more confident of himself than I was.

I pulled away only when I felt the need to breathe. I didn't pull far away though, only so much so that our lips were close but not touching.

Josh's eyes fluttered open, and we stared at each other. We were so close our noses bumped together, so close I could feel his warm breath on my own lips.

This was new, and instead of being terrifying as I'd always thought it would be—it was exciting.

"I like you," he whispered. His eyes were staring into mine while he said it, without even blinking, so he couldn't be lying.

"How *can* you?" I asked, confused and excited all at once. "You don't know me."

"You don't have to know a person to like him. To be in love with him, yes, but not to be attracted to him."

That was... true. After all, wasn't I attracted to him too? I didn't know him any better than he knew me.

"We could get to know each other. I would like that."

"What would that entail?" Why couldn't I just say yes? I *did* want to get to know him.

"I don't know." He pulled back further, and I experienced an intense need to pull him back in close. I didn't though, just watched him silently. "More of what we just did, hopefully."

I swallowed. "So you want a relationship?"

He blinked, suddenly uncertain. Maybe that was my fault, because of all my questions. "Yes?"

I cocked my head to the side. "You're not sure?"

He pulled even further away from me. "If you don't want to, all you have to do is say so." He stood up, shoved his bowl of popcorn at me then brushed past me with his journal pressed tightly to his chest.

"Josh—" *What the hell?*

"Just don't!" His voice was thick, and he continued walking to the edge of the row. "It's okay. I get it. I wouldn't want to get to know me either." And with that he bolted.

I was shocked.

What had caused such an extreme reaction in him?

He was high and he was low and definitely not somewhere in-between, not ever. Either he was really sad, or he was really happy. Wasn't there some sort of middle-ground?

And what the heck was I supposed to do with a bowl of popcorn I hadn't even wanted in the first place?

I threw it in the rubbish as I left the cinema.

AUGUST 6TH

I messed it up. It had such good potential and then I messed it up.

No, wait, he messed it up. What was he asking all those questions for? He didn't want it, I could tell. And I'd liked him so much. Kind, handsome, and he'd seemed to like me too... Only he didn't.

Why can't anyone ever just like me for me?

Why can't I ever be good enough?

Why doesn't he like me?

What did I do wrong?

AUGUST 7TH

I am so embarrassed.

There's no excuse for the way I acted last night. I'm not sure anymore if he was rejecting me. I think he might've not been, you know? I don't know. I don't read people well.

Vincent says I have this black-and-white mentality. That it's a standard thinking pattern for my diagnosis. That the embarrassment and shame is too. But I still feel. All of it. It's so all-consuming, I don't even know what to do.

So I cut. That's what I do right?

Cut. Cut. Cut.

I can't even stop. Can't ever quit. Quitting would kill me because the cutting is what keeps me grounded. Mostly, anyway. Or no, not even mostly. Sometimes.

One wrong word, one question too much, and I fly off the handle.

I hate myself.

I hate myself so much.

How can I ever expect him to like me when I can't even like myself?

CHAPTER 6

JOSH

$\mathcal{I}$ was in therapy four days a week. Two days with Vincent, just the two of us, and then two days of group therapy with other people who had deep issues like me.

Group therapy wasn't new to me—I'd had to participate in it when I'd been hospitalised too—but these people were. I couldn't seem to get comfortable around them, nor had I with the members of the group in the hospital.

I preferred one-on-one conversations, but Vincent thought group was a good idea and so did my mum. Though she tended to agree with Vincent on most things, him being a professional and all.

When I walked in the door, I was sure I was the first person to arrive, until I saw Mal sitting huddled on the chair furthest away from the door. He was wearing his standard baggy clothes. His jumper was so big he could draw the sleeves down to cover his hands entirely, bunch the fabric in his palms, and still not have stretched the fabric out much. He also had the hood up and his head bowed, and I knew he was having a bad day.

"Hey, Mal." I sunk down on the chair next to him.

Mal was the person who had experiences most resembling my own. We had a lot in common, him and me, when it came to our pasts and our current inability to stop mutilating our own bodies. We even shared the same diagnosis.

One eye peeked up at me. "Hey," he muttered. His voice was low and hoarse, like he'd been crying. Or screaming. Either was likely. I knew from my own experience.

"All right?" I knew he wasn't. I could see he wasn't. But I didn't know what else to say. I'd never actually spoken to Mal before, outside of the group circle.

He didn't answer me though. He didn't have to.

And I didn't say anything else. I just clutched my journal to my chest and sunk down further on the chair.

I never used to be early for group because I was afraid of situations like these. The awkward ones where I had to make small talk. I didn't do small talk. I messed things up with that.

But everything had been a mess of people at home. My cousins were too much, and I'd left just to get some peace and quiet.

Though the noise sure could help dull my own thoughts. The embarrassment and the shame still sat deep after last night. I didn't know what to do about it. Doing nothing would mean continuing feeling like this, but actually doing something… then I'd have to face it. I didn't think I could.

People were starting to arrive now, and I heard Mal heave a sigh next to me as the room began to fill. Maybe we even felt the same about group therapy. Maybe we had a lot more than just our pasts in common.

I wanted to speak to him.

The sudden feeling, the need, to get to know him better was overwhelming. He knew—he understood. He wouldn't judge me, no matter what. Because we were so much alike. We both even had blond hair, though I was pretty sure he had brown eyes instead of green ones.

I cast around for something to say, but it was too late now. There were other people here, which meant Mal would prefer to talk as little as possible. So would I, for that matter.

I didn't like group. It was too many people.

I didn't do well when things got to be too much.

～

I was halfway on my way to Soho before I realised the direction I was going.

I stood on a street corner, anxious about which choice to make. I'd been brave yesterday. I'd gone to his job to see him.

I wasn't so brave today.

I headed back home.

The house was quiet when I entered, and I let out the breath I hadn't even known I was holding. I stepped out of my shoes and shrugged out of my jacket, then put them in their proper place before heading towards my bedroom.

When I opened the door and a dark shadow sat up straight in my bed, my heart nearly beat a path out of my chest.

"Hey, cousin." Cooper grinned at me, all mischievous. A bottle dangled from two of his fingers, and when I peered at it, I saw it was Vodka.

"What are you doing?" I switched the overhead light on so I could see better and then took a tentative step inside.

"Waiting for you." Cooper moved around on my bed until he was sitting cross-legged.

We were alike, Cooper and I. It was easy to see we were cousins. He had his mother's looks, and my aunt was the spitting image of my own mum, who I got my looks from. The only differences were the shape of his face, his blue eyes, and the fact that he was a couple of inches taller than me.

And he didn't have arms covered in scars.

I closed the door behind me and went over to sit on my desk chair. "Anything special?" I hadn't spoken much to Cooper since they'd all arrived. Cooper kept to himself, and whenever I'd been home, I'd been surrounded by the rest of the family.

"We're leaving on Sunday. I just thought we could spend some time together before then, you know? I had this brilliant idea that you need to get your mind off of stuff, so I nicked this from your mother's cabinet." He tilted the bottle towards me. "I was thinking we could go out tonight. Get smashed out of our wits."

Now that was a good idea. Alcohol worked just as well to dull the senses as cutting. It even lasted longer.

Cooper held the bottle out to me.

I took it.

CHAPTER 7

DAMIAN

*W*hy had I said yes to dinner?

I'd regretted it the moment I walked in the door of my uncle and aunt's house, when it turned out Chloe had brought her new girl-friend over to meet the family.

Chloe and I were the same age. She was my aunt's sister; I was my uncle's nephew, but we'd grown up together in this house. If I were more receptive to other people, I'd go so far as to say we were like siblings because we honestly should've been.

But I wasn't very receptive to other people, and she didn't understand me, and so we had absolutely nothing in common. That didn't mean I didn't love her, because I did. We just didn't have much to say to each other.

I hadn't even known Chloe was bisexual, and now here I was, faced with another woman. She wasn't as feminine as Chloe, more of a tomboy perhaps. She seemed okay. Less energetic than Chloe, anyway, which was always a plus in my book. Chloe could exhaust me sometimes.

Dinner was an affair in itself. Everyone was talking around me.

Ray and Claire, my uncle and aunt, conversed with Chloe and Quinn, trying their best to be open and friendly, getting to know Quinn better. Mathilda and Matthew, my young cousins, were talking amongst themselves, and sometimes breaking into the adults' conversation.

It all gave me a headache. I was glad when dinner was over and the two children were sent off to watch the telly in the living room.

I wondered how long I would have to stay. When could I leave without it being rude? Again, I had no idea, because this wasn't a situation I'd ever been in before.

I should text Silver. He would know.

"Damian." Chloe turned to me. She smiled widely and her eyes were practically shining.

She's happy, I realised. I wondered if I would ever

be so obviously happy about anything. Certainly not with Josh, as that seemed to have ended before it even started.

"What?" I moved on my chair, trying to find a comfortable position. I couldn't find one.

"Quinn and I are going out later. I think you should join us." She didn't phrase it as a question because she knew I'd just say no then.

"Why?" I frowned, suspicious all of a sudden.

Chloe never asked me to go out with her. She had a life she enjoyed, a social one, whereas I was the loner who never got close to anyone. We were like night and day: we didn't go together.

"Because you seem down. You've hardly said a word all evening. Maybe it'll cheer you up? If not, at least you'll get out for a bit." Her smile wasn't as wide anymore, but it was still directed at me. It was eerie. People hardly ever smiled at me.

I didn't particularly want to go out. But what else did I have? To go home to my bedroom and bury myself in some book? That wasn't exactly alluring at the moment either.

"On one condition," I said, and once she raised her eyebrows in question, I continued, "If I can ask Silver to come too."

It might be cowardly, but I didn't want to go out to some pub or club without my best friend. He was the sociable one of the two of us, but he was also loyal. He wouldn't leave me all alone, like I was pretty sure Chloe would once she got a few drinks in her and met people she knew. She wasn't the type of person to stick to my lonesome side all night.

Her smile widened. "Of course. Silver is great!"

I knew they knew each other. They weren't close, but ever since Chloe started her trainee-period as a hairdresser, Silver had gone to her to get his hair cut. I usually preferred to go to someone I didn't know, but maybe going to Chloe would make her happy? Silver was adamant she was good.

I shot off a text to Silver, hoping he would say no. If he said no, I could back out of it. I wasn't about to go anywhere with Chloe and her girlfriend by myself.

Sadly, he was free and more than happy to come along.

Why couldn't anything ever go my way?

CHAPTER 8

DAMIAN

*T*he club was crowded, loud, and stuffy. Everything I'd anticipated before we'd even gone out.

It wasn't my scene at all.

I never went out because I knew I didn't like it, that I wouldn't be comfortable. I preferred to stay in my comfort zone, thank you very much.

"Cheer up, mate." Silver bumped my shoulder with his. "It's only one night. You can do all your regular boring stuff every other night."

I glowered at him. "This is your scene. Not mine."

He grinned widely. "And it's a wonderful scene too!" His eyes strayed, and then he nodded. I turned to see what he was directing my attention towards. I couldn't pin-point anything out of the ordinary. "See that green-haired bloke at the bar over there?"

Now that he mentioned green hair... yes, I did see him. Small, petite, with *green* hair. "What about him?" I eyed him suspiciously. Who dyed their hair *green*?

"He's Chloe's workmate." Silver couldn't take his eyes off the bloke.

"He's the reason you said yes to go out with them?"

"Not at all. He's just a bonus." He turned his focus back to me. "I don't think he knows me though."

"Get Chloe to introduce you then," I said, like it was the easiest thing in the world. It had to be, right? He knew Chloe; Chloe knew what's-his-name. What was the big deal? I didn't know Silver to be shy.

"Maybe I will." His focus was drawn over my shoulder and his grin fell away. "Hey, D, isn't that your bloke?"

"What?" I grimaced.

When he continued to stare over my shoulder, I turned around to follow his line of sight and found he was right.

Not that Josh could be called mine in any kind of sense, but it was him.

He was leaning against the wall and seemed to

be struggling to straighten up. He took a step forward, instantly stumbled, and leant back against the wall.

I took a step towards him, worried.

He seemed to have trouble keeping his eyes open too.

When he suddenly fell to his knees, I was at his side in an instant.

"Josh?" I touched his shoulders tentatively, not at all sure my touch would be welcome.

He lifted his head with great struggle and peered up at me. "H-hey." He even had trouble talking.

"He's smashed, D." Silver was at my side, also crouched down. "Better get him outside." I nodded jerkily and together we got Josh up on his feet and out of the club.

"Cooper," Josh mumbled.

"What?" I turned my head to look at him.

"Cooper's in there."

"Who's Cooper?" Something big and dark flashed through me, and I let go of him.

Silver wasn't prepared, and Josh crashed to the ground.

"Shit!" I kneeled down, guilty I had let him go in the first place. "Are you all right?"

Josh groaned and cradled his head in his arms.

I looked up at Silver for help. I had no idea what

to do. I'd never dealt with anyone who was drunk before.

"You should get him home." Silver could clearly see my panic. "Get him to drink a lot of water, then put him to bed. He needs to sleep it off."

"You mean take him to our place?" I frowned.

"Yeah, why not? He needs to be looked after." Silver took his mobile out and pressed a few buttons. "I'll call you a taxi."

"Wha—wait!" But he didn't listen to me. Instead he stood up and walked a few feet away to talk.

I looked back down at Josh, who was groaning. I rubbed his back.

I wasn't sure he'd appreciate being taken back to my place, not with me. Not after the way last night had ended. But I couldn't leave him either, not in the state he was in.

Not after the way something had jolted in me when he'd mentioned another bloke's name.

Was that jealousy?

It was the first time I'd felt anything like it.

"Taxi'll be here in a minute." Silver was back at our side. "You want me to go back with you?"

"I don't know." I kept rubbing Josh's back, hoping it would soothe me just as much as him.

I had no idea what I was doing, what I was supposed to do.

Silver must have sensed it or seen it. "I'll go back with you."

I lifted my head. "Don't you have a green-haired bloke to woo?"

He chuckled. "I can do that some other day. He's not going anywhere." Silver crouched back down so we were at eye-level. "This is more important now."

I couldn't even begin to say how grateful I was.

A little over a year ago now, on the first day of my last year in college, he'd sat down next to me at lunch and that had been it. I couldn't even say how exactly we'd got talking, but we'd been friends since. And he really was a good friend.

I didn't need anyone else as long as I had Silver; I doubted someone else could ever fill the role of best friend as well as he did.

The taxi pulled up eventually and we both had to struggle to get Josh into the car. He leaned against me on the drive home, halfway asleep. He protested weakly when we had to get him out of the car again and into the flat.

"I'll get him some water," Silver said once we'd put him down on the sofa.

Josh had lain down, eyes closed, but they fluttered open slightly now to look at me where I stood next to him, uncertain what to do. "You know what's wrong with me?"

"Uh, no." I wasn't sure if it was a question he expected an answer to or not. An answer I should know. Because I had no idea.

"They say I've got brain damage. Severe brain damage. It's like I've got third-degree burns in my mind." He touched his head with a shaking hand. "Brain damage. Like I've been hit in the head or something. But I haven't. He's ruined me. Not just my body but my *mind*. How's that even possible?" A few tears slipped from his eyes and trickled down his temples into his hair.

I frowned again now and sat down on the edge of the table. *Brain damage*? I never would've guessed he had such a serious condition. I couldn't know for sure how smart he was, but he seemed like a normal bloke at first glance, unless I counted the swinging moods.

"I feel everything so much deeper and longer and more intensely than normal people. Apparently I have a way of thinking in black-and-white. What does that even mean?" More tears trickled, and he turned his head away to face the back of the sofa. "My emotions are all over the place. You know what they call it?"

I shook my head, trying to digest everything he was saying. How could he go from a stuttering mess at the club to suddenly sharing all of this? Maybe he just really needed to talk to someone and the alcohol brought it out more easily. "No."

"Borderline personality disorder." He sniffled. "Not just a mental illness, but bloody *brain damage.* Or are all mental illnesses brain damage?" He squeezed his eyes shut, forcing more tears to trickle. "I don't know. I don't know. I don't want this. I never asked for it. Not once."

I had a feeling his last words weren't about the disorder or the brain damage, but I couldn't know for certain because he'd stopped talking now. He trembled, arms wrapped around himself.

"Here." A glass of water was thrust in front of my face.

I looked up at Silver.

He stared down at me, eyes dark and swirling. He'd heard. He must've.

"Get him to drink that. All of it. I'll go get a bucket in case he gets sick during the night."

I nodded then focused back on Josh as Silver went to the bathroom. I managed to prop him up a bit, and I put the glass to his lips, tilting it carefully.

He gulped it down slowly, but down it went.

When the glass was empty, I put it on the table and pushed Josh further up into a sitting position.

Silver was back and together we got him into my

room and in my bed. He rolled over to face the wall, and I tucked the duvet around him.

"I'll go get some more water," I told him, not sure if he was listening or not. "I'll be back soon."

Silver and I exited my room, and I ran my hand over my face in frustration once we were back in the living room.

"Shit."

"That's the proper word, all right."

I plucked the glass up from the table. "You heard it all, right?"

"Sure did." Silver braced his hands against the back of the sofa. "That's some heavy shit, D."

"You know about that disorder? Borderline?"

"Not really. I mean, V talks about a lot of that stuff whenever we meet, but I never put any of it to memory. Psychology is his field, not mine. But I imagine it's *bad*. Even the word is intimidating. Borderline." He shook his head. "I can ask him about it tomorrow, if you want?"

I nodded. "Is it wrong that I like him?" If he could ask his brother about the diagnosis, I could figure more out. I needed to know what I was getting into. It must be some kind of mood disorder, considering how easily Josh's mood changed. I still had no idea what had set him off last night.

"Of course it isn't." Silver didn't look reassuring

though, and I raised my eyebrows in question. "I just think you need to be absolutely certain that you do want him before you let yourself get involved. Mental illnesses… They're not easy to navigate, you know. I don't know the particulars of this one, but people dealing with mental illness are usually pretty frail. They can't take much."

"I know." I glanced at my bedroom door. My mind flashed back to the cinema the night before, but I still couldn't pinpoint exactly what had gone wrong. "I never thought this would happen."

Silver finally grinned again. "Love, mate, it happens unexpectedly."

"Love," I snorted, unbelieving. "I've known him two days."

"Attraction then. Whatever. Love always starts somewhere, you know." Silver came around the sofa to clap me on the shoulder. "You okay from here? Now that we're home, I'm just going to head to bed."

I nodded. "Yeah. Thanks for this." We hadn't even made it to the club properly before we'd had to leave. He hadn't even got a drink. And I hadn't told Chloe we'd left. "Chloe. We didn't tell her we left."

"I'll text her," Silver offered. "You go take care of your bloke."

I went to refill the glass before I headed into the bedroom. I put it down on the bedside table, then grabbed my pyjamas and went to the bathroom to change and brush my teeth.

Josh was still facing the wall when I got back. He was trembling.

"Hey, you all right?"

"C-cold." His teeth chattered.

I sat back on my knees. I only had my two duvets, so I put my own over him too.

Not that it seemed to help much.

When he continued to tremble, I slipped under both duvets too and pressed up against his back. Wasn't bodily contact best, after all?

"This okay?" I rested my cheek against his soft, blond hair.

"Y-yeah." He was still shaking, but he gripped my hand as if it was a lifeline.

I wish I could say I lay awake for a long time, making sure he was okay, but I didn't. I fell rather hurriedly asleep.

CHAPTER 9

JOSH

I woke to a head that throbbed and a throat that felt like sandpaper.

And to a wall that definitely wasn't mine.

I tensed up immediately, casting about for what exactly had happened last night. I couldn't remember. I couldn't remember anything past arriving at the club with Cooper.

Oh no, no, no.

Had I gone home with someone?

I moved tentatively. The mattress moved with me easily, so there didn't seem to be anyone in bed with me.

I rolled over very slowly, dreading what I would find.

The bed was empty, except for me.

And I was wearing my clothes. They weren't haphazardly strewn on the floor like they would've been if I'd been in a mood to go on the pull last night.

The bedside table looked familiar.

I lifted my head to take in the rest of the room. All familiar.

Damian.

I'd gone home with him? That would certainly explain why I still had my clothes on, as he wasn't interested in a shag.

There was a glass full of water on the bedside table and I grabbed it, drinking greedily. I hoped it had been left there for me because I finished the glass in two long swallows.

Once I put it back, I sat for a while not knowing what to do. I had no idea where Damian was or what mood he was in. Or what I'd done last night. Had I come here, all drunk and desperate?

I dreaded finding out what humiliating act had led to me sleeping in his bed.

I rose from the bed and walked across the floor. I figured it would be better to find out right there and then instead of wondering about it, imagining all kinds of scenarios.

The door squeaked a bit as I opened it, which brought my attention to someone moving on the sofa.

Damian had sat forward so he could look at the door and our eyes met.

My breath caught at the sight of him, both because I was very much attracted to him, but also because of the humiliation of the way we'd parted two nights ago—and possible shame for what I'd done to end up here last night.

"Hey," he said, voice low and calm. He didn't seem angry or upset or disappointed or distressed. Just… normal.

"Hey." I shut the bedroom door after me and then padded across the floor to the sofa.

He scooted over to make room for me.

I sat down as far away from him as possible, pressed against the arm of the sofa. I was hungover, and I must look it and smell like it.

"You all right?"

I shrugged. "As well as can be expected, I guess." I dreaded asking the questions I knew needed to be answered. It was better for me not to know, but at the same time, not knowing was driving me mad.

"Do you want some painkillers? Might make you feel better."

"Yes, please."

He went to get them, and I was left to my own scattered thoughts.

He came back with two painkillers and a new glass of water.

I took both gratefully and downed the pills in quick succession.

Damian sunk down next to me again. He was still so very calm. Maybe too calm?

"About last night," I started. "If I did something or said something inappropriate, I'm sorry. I do a lot of shit when I'm drunk I would never do if I were sober."

"You didn't do anything."

"Then how did I end up here?"

"I met you at the club last night. You don't remember?"

I shook my head. I couldn't remember a thing after arriving.

"I suppose you wouldn't." He smiled now. "You were smashed. Silver and I brought you home. I couldn't leave you there."

I blinked several times. "Really? Not even after the way I left you the other night?"

"Who knows what could've happened to you if you'd stayed there." He wasn't so calm anymore as he fiddled with the hem of his jumper.

"Yeah," I murmured, turning my head away.

We sat in heavy silence for several minutes.

"Look, about the other night... I don't know what

I said to upset you, but I didn't mean to. I would like to get to know you too."

My heart started beating heavily. "You mean that?"

"Of course I do. I wouldn't have said it otherwise."

I chanced a glance his way. He still fiddled with the hem of his jumper. "I'm sorry for the way I left. I just thought—" Thought? Had I been thinking at all? "I thought you didn't want it. That I was the only one."

"You're not."

Those two words did something to me. Something I was unfamiliar with: they made me feel *happy*. I couldn't remember the last time that feeling had lodged in my chest like it did now.

Probably never.

"You said some things last night—" The happy feeling was instantly squashed by his hesitant words. "About your diagnosis. Borderline. I don't know anything about it, but from what you said... it can't be easy being you."

I swallowed heavily. "What did I say?" *I don't want to know, I don't want to know, I don't want to—*

"Nothing bad. You just kind of laid it all out there for me." He glanced at me with a barely-there smile.

"I'm glad you did. I guess I understand you a bit better now. Not much, but a bit."

I managed a tentative smile in return. "You don't mind?"

"No. I don't." He seemed thoughtful and surprised, like the words surprised even him.

They sure surprised me. Even though I was a mess, with a severe mental illness, he still wanted to get to know me.

I wanted to touch him, hug him, and kiss him and show him exactly how much his words meant to me. That he gave me a chance, even with everything against us—with my psyche against us—meant more to me than I could articulate with words.

But I was still hungover after yesterday's drinking binge, and alcohol breath together with morning breath… Probably not a good idea to get any closer to him than I already was.

"Can I use the bathroom?" I needed to get cleaned up as best I could.

He nodded, then leant forward and grabbed a small plastic bag from the table. "I went down to Tesco earlier and got this for you."

"T-thanks." I took it and clutched it close.

As soon as I was in the bathroom, I opened it to see what it was: a toothbrush, more painkillers, toothpaste, floss, and deodorant. That happy feeling flashed through me again, so foreign I stayed still to enjoy if for a moment.

He was so kind, so caring.

I fixed myself up to my best extent.

Damian was still on the sofa when I came back out.

"I've got today off," he said.

"Yeah?" I had no idea what he wanted to imply with that statement.

"Maybe we could do something? If you don't have anything else you need to do?"

"Yes! I mean, no. I don't have anything else that requires my attention." I hadn't blown it the other night. The relief was palpable, like an iron weight had been lifted off my chest.

"I was thinking maybe we could head out to Camden. To the Markets." He shrugged, looking unsure, like it wasn't a good idea.

I nodded enthusiastically. "That sounds great. I love the Camden Markets."

"Should we go now?"

"Yeah, why not?" There was no point sitting around, after all. "Should we take the bus?" I asked once we were outside.

"Why not the tube?"

"Isn't that a bit expensive?"

He glanced at me. "Right. You're not working."

"That's not what I mean." I shook my head. "I was thinking about you. You're working to pay rent on your flat and probably to save up for when you start school. Don't worry about me. Mum's born into money, so I'm not exactly lacking in that department."

One blink of his eyes told me his surprise. "I don't mind the tube. I can afford it. It's quicker, anyway."

"Okay then."

Tube it was.

We didn't say much. I didn't know what to say, exactly, and maybe he didn't either.

We arrived in Camden and walked up the bustling streets towards the Markets.

I'd been truthful when I said I loved the Markets, but I also loved Camden itself. In Camden, more than any other place, people were themselves: Goths, punk, whatever style people preferred. It wasn't unusual to see someone with an orange mohawk walking around Camden in clothes that resembled bondage gear.

It wasn't my style, but I sure could appreciate it on someone else. How they dared to be themselves no matter what.

"Are the painkillers working?"

"Mm, yeah." The throbbing had been decidedly less pronounced for a while now.

"Maybe we should get some food?"

We crossed the road, started into the Market, and first came upon where all the food was being offered. I wasn't feeling particularly hungry, but I also hadn't eaten in… I couldn't remember when I'd last eaten. So food was definitely a necessity.

We got a few of those marinated chicken-breasts on skewers. I had no idea what they were called, but they tasted good.

I tried to eat as carefully as possible so I wouldn't embarrass myself in front of him, and I did pretty well. I didn't spill anything on myself, at least.

We continued through the Market after we finished eating. The clothing shops weren't for either of us since it was either women's dresses or alternative clothes, so we passed right by them.

A booth selling various bracelets and assorted jewellery caught my attention. Especially the rainbow-coloured rubber bands.

"You know what these are?" I held one up for Damian to see.

He gave me a look that clearly said he didn't.

I chuckled. "Rainbow bands. It's to show you're gay." At least that was the only thing I'd ever heard they were used for. "Cooper has several of these on both of his arms."

"Cooper, right." Damian buried his hands in his pockets and hunched his shoulders.

I watched him, confused, and he turned his head away from me. "Did I tell him I left last night?" He shook his head. "Shit." I hadn't brought my phone with me. Mum must be beside herself by now.

"If he really cared, wouldn't he be the one to take care of you?" Damian snapped, and my head shot up to stare at him again. "You were left to your own devices."

"That's typical of Cooper. He likes to party." I put the rubber bracelet down and went to stand in front of Damian. "Hey… What's wrong?" He hunched his shoulders up further. Whatever it was, he didn't want to tell me. "Damian. Did I say something wrong?"

He refused to look at me. "Were you planning on going home with him last night? Cooper?"

"Well, yeah."

Hurt flashed over his face, and I realised suddenly what was going on.

"Cooper's my cousin," I hurried to say. I didn't like seeing Damian hurt, and the quicker I could get that look off his face, the quicker we could get past this misunderstanding and go back to having a good time. "He's staying with us, with his family. I went out with him last night because he thought I needed it. I did need to get out, to stop thinking about everything, but I shouldn't have drunk so much."

"Cousin?" He fixated on that small part.

"Yeah. Cousin." I smiled. "We look a lot alike, too."

The hurt was replaced with a sheepish expression, and Damian ducked his head to cover it. Didn't matter, as I'd already seen it. I turned back to the bracelets, letting him get himself together without me looking at him.

"I'm getting a few of these. Maybe I can wear them once I take the gauze off."

"You have anyone you need to advertise your gayness to?"

That brought forth a chuckle. "You want one?" I turned and held one up. "They're rather flashy and nice-looking, aren't they?"

He eyed it with distaste. "No thanks."

I paid for three of them, then went back to join him. "You're a pretty private person, aren't you?"

He shrugged. "I don't want people knowing my business."

We continued down the street. Our shoulders bumped together as we had to walk close due to all the other people bustling around us.

"Thank you," I said eventually. "For taking care

of me last night, for taking me home and for this morning. For this *moment*. It means a lot to me."

"Don't mention it."

He flashed me a small smile, and I knew he was telling the truth. He didn't mind, about last night or me being a mess. He didn't mind it at all—he just wanted to spend time with me.

And the feeling that left...

It couldn't even be described.

CHAPTER 10

"*J*oshua!"

Mum was on me the moment I stepped through the door. Her arms wrapped around my shoulders and she pressed her cheek against the side of my head.

I was surrounded by her hair and her perfume and it was both overwhelming and calming. We never really hugged, but she hugged me now, and it felt good.

"Where have you been?" She drew back eventually and held me an arm's length out from her. "Cooper said you went out together last night, but then you disappeared. He couldn't find you." Her eyes searched my face frantically, then her hands ran over my shoulders and down my arms, until she gripped my forearms.

I flinched away from that. They might be wrapped up and not giving me much pain, but when she squeezed like that, it came flashing back.

"Joshua." Her hands clenched into fists as she gazed down at my arms. I knew they were covered up, but her stare made me want to hide my arms behind my back. It was like she could see right through both my jumper and the gauze.

"I'm fine, Mum." I was more than fine, actually. I'd had the most wonderful day of my entire life.

Only thing I was sad about was that it had ended and I was back home.

I hadn't wanted to leave him, but I had to go home to avoid Mum calling the police. She would've, if she hadn't heard from me soon.

Since she found out, two years ago, she'd become rather over-protective. I didn't mind, usually, because we'd grown so much closer since my suicide attempt.

"Where have you been?"

"With a friend." To think that I could actually say that out loud and it wasn't a lie.

Her eyebrows drew together. "A friend?" I could tell she didn't believe me.

"I can have those, you know," I snapped, my

mood doing a quick turn-over. "He's the only one, but he *is* my friend."

The frown disappeared, but it was replaced by a sad expression. "Of course you can have friends, Joshua. It was just the first I'd heard of it, was all." She turned away, towards the kitchen. "Will you come with me for a bit? I want to talk to you about something."

I followed her, cautious. What could she possibly want to talk about?

"Where are the others?" The flat was silent for once.

"They went out." Mum texted something on her phone. She caught me looking at it, suspicious now. "I'm just letting Mother know you're home. She's been worried sick about you too. They all have."

"They don't have to worry. I'm fine." I sunk down on one of the kitchen chairs, and she took the one opposite me. Again I could tell she didn't believe me, and I was instantly miffed again. "As fine as I can be."

I'd folded my hands on the table and she reached over now to cover them with her own. "This is hard for all of us, but *especially* for you. I can't imagine what you're thinking now."

No, she couldn't. She'd never had the satisfaction of seeing her abuser put behind bars. But once she found out, she'd been relentless in putting Andrew behind them.

To protect me.

She'd left me in his care only to find out he hadn't really cared for me at all.

I was aware of her sitting in front of me, her blonde hair cut into a straight bob, but I could also see her with her hair longer, past her shoulder, and her eyes filled with tears.

"I'm so sorry."

I tilted my head in her direction. "What're you sorry for?"

"For not seeing the signs." She turned her head away so I couldn't look at her anymore. "I should've seen the signs of what was going on, of what he was doing to you."

"He was very careful not to let you know." My lap had become very interesting all of a sudden.

"I still should've seen them. I should've seen the signs better than anyone." Her hands were balled into fists, gripping the fabric of her trousers in-between them.

Those words held meaning, I could feel it. "What do you mean?" My voice shook.

She hesitated with her answer, and I could see the internal struggle going on due to the rapid changes in her expression. Even in profile they were obvious.

"I've never told anyone this before, and now I'm sitting here, telling you. I know I haven't been a good mum for you, that I've left you to your own devices — to him — and that I've been largely absent. I am so sorry about that. I never meant to be absent from your life, to not even know you. For sixteen years I ignored my own son, leaving him in the single care of my husband while I focused on my career. It's no excuse though to ignore you, it really isn't. I am so ashamed, and all I can do is tell you how sorry I am and how much I want to make it up to you. If that's even possible at this point."

I heard what she was saying, every word of it, but my mind had stuck on her first sentence and I couldn't let it go. "What'd you mean? What've you never told anyone?" My voice still shook, but it also demanded answers. I needed to know.

She glanced up at me, but when our eyes met, she quickly turned away again. "I should've seen the signs because — " She took a shaky breath. "Because I've been exactly where you are, Joshua."

My eyes widened. "W-what?"

"I've been a victim of sexual abuse too." She closed her eyes as if she was in pain. She probably was. I knew better than anyone just how much the inside could hurt. I bet talking about it had her remembering it all over again and I shuddered at the thought.

I couldn't take my eyes off her. I was frozen in place. "You? But—Who? Who did that to you?"

She pressed her lips together into a small line. "My father." It came out as a bitter snarl, like the word was the worst of curses. "For four very long years he did things to me. Then he was diagnosed with cancer and died. Months of pain were what he got, because the cancer had already spread and there was nothing they could do. I didn't feel sorry for him. I was happy he was suffering. Karma had come back and properly bitch-slapped him in the face. He got what he deserved, and when he died, I was happy then too. I would never have to see his face again, I would never have him crawling into my bed."

My throat had gone dry. "How old were you?"

"From when I was ten until I was fourteen."

Four years of violation. Not even half of my ten, but it was still four years too much. At least Andrew wasn't related to me by blood. He was just my stepfather. She'd been violated by her very own dad, the man whose genes she shared.

"Does Grandma know?"

She looked back at me, eyes a dark green. "No. And she never will. Promise me you'll never tell her, Joshua. You're the only one I've ever told. Not even Abbi—my own sister—knows what a bastard of a father we had.

Knowing this would destroy Mother and she doesn't deserve that."

"I won't tell." I understood her, because I hadn't wanted anyone to know about my circumstances either. But once I'd woken up and had been told I would be fine, that I would have no damage from the pills and that I would be able to go back home... I'd lost it. I couldn't go back home when he would be there.

And mum had been there. She'd listened, with tears trickling, and now I finally got to hear her story.

She turned to me again. "It saddens me that I've shut you out so completely you didn't feel like you could ever come to me with this. I never had time—I didn't care enough—to get to know you properly, so I never even imagined anything was wrong. I'm so sorry, Joshua." The tears were overflowing now, trickling slowly down her cheeks.

"It's okay. I didn't want you to know. I didn't want anyone to know." I was so ashamed and humiliated. Used as my own stepfather's blow-up doll and punching bag for ten years, and then failing at committing suicide when I'd finally had enough. When I couldn't take it anymore.

"Joshua!"
I was startled out of the memory, or flashback, or

whatever it was called when the present just fell away from me. "Mum?"

Her eyes searched my face again, alert and worried. "You spaced out. For a long time."

"I'm sorry, I was just—" My head felt fuzzy and I pressed my hands to my temples, hoping it would settle down. "Remembering. I was just remembering something."

She took a deep breath. "You do that sometimes. Like you just check out for a bit. It scares me."

She just used the same word Damian did. Back when he'd witnessed it, I'd been remembering Andrew though, not my mother telling me of her own abusive past. "I'm okay."

"Are you really though?" She leant forward, gaze fixed on me.

I twitched in discomfort. "What'd you mean?"

"I don't think you are okay." Her hands clenched and unclenched on the table in front of her. "You know Mother and the rest of them are leaving Sunday, right?"

I nodded. Where was she going with this conversation?

"I think you should go with them?"

In even less than a blink of an eye, she'd ruined everything. "You want to send me away?" I stood up so quickly my chair fell with a crash to the floor.

"You want to be rid of me again? Hospitalisation wasn't enough, now you want to ship me off to Bristol too?"

"Joshua, no, that's not—"

I stormed out of the kitchen and slammed my bedroom door behind me, then locked it to be certain she wouldn't come in.

I paced the floor, since I didn't know what else to do.

She wanted to send me away. I'd just come home not long ago, and already she was tired of me. How could she do that to me? Didn't she understand? I just wanted her to love me—to want me there with her!

I became aware I was hitting myself. Stomach, chest, head. Hitting myself everywhere I could reach.

It wasn't enough. It didn't *hurt*.

I tore the room apart looking for something sharp. Books on my desk were shoved to the floor, my nightstand was upended in my hurry to get the drawer out. Once I found a razor, one of those small yet deadly sharp ones, I pulled my shirt sleeve up and ripped off the gauze.

I didn't even feel it. I could see my fingers holding it, could see it cutting into skin, slashing over it and leaving trails of blood in its wake. But I didn't *feel* it. Why couldn't I *feel* it?

"Joshua!" Mum knocked frantically on my door. I could hear her sobbing. "Open up! Joshua, please!"

Cut, cut, cut.

Feel, feel, feel.

Except I didn't.

I didn't feel it.

My chest hurt, my head hurt, but nothing on the outside. The outside was numb, dead.

I screamed.

I wasn't sure if I did it out loud or if I just did it in my head, but it had me on my knees on the floor, bending over until I had my face buried in the crook of my elbows.

Blood was everywhere; on my arms, on my face, in my hair, on the floor.

And I still didn't feel it.

CHAPTER 11

DAMIAN

*S*ilver was on the sofa, sprawled out, with his head resting against the back of it. He seemed to be deep in thought.

"Hey," I said, hoping I wouldn't startle him. Though opening and closing the front door should've done that in the first place.

He blinked, then slowly tilted his head further back so he could see me. "Hey. I might've done something today that's not exactly ethically correct."

"What are you talking about?" I wrestled my trainers off and put them away, then shrugged out of my thin summer jacket.

"Chloe texted me today. She wants to get a tattoo done. I told her I'd do it for free one night, after work, if she would bring Kian."

"Kian?" That name did not ring a bell.

"The green-haired bloke I pointed out to you last night?"

"Oh. Right." I went to sit down on the two-seater.

"That's all you've got to say?" He'd lifted his head off the back of the sofa now so he could continue to watch me.

"Is there anything else to say?"

"I just bribed Chloe with a free tattoo so she'd bring a bloke I like. A bloke I haven't even spoken to before." Silver ran his hands over his face. "Does it get more pathetic than that?"

"You're asking the wrong person, mate."

"Not anymore, I'm not." His lips split into a grin. "How was your day?"

"Fine." I tried not to look at him, but his scrutiny made it hard.

"Where've you been?"

"The Camden Markets."

"With that bloke of yours?"

"His name is Josh. And yeah." It had been a nice day. I'd managed to get through it without saying anything that sent him running, like the last time. That was progress.

"About him. I stopped by V's office after work and we had a little chat."

"Yeah?" My interest was piqued now and I leaned forward. "What'd he have to say?"

"A lot. He gave me a few links to relevant websites." Silver reached into his pocket and produced a folded up note. I took it, but I didn't open it. "What I said last night, about you needing to be sure... You do, D. This is heavy shit. You need to be absolutely committed to it."

Before, I would say I wasn't.

But now... I did like Josh, a lot. He drew me in like no one else ever had, even if he had his faults.

But once I read up on his disorder, I was pretty sure those faults weren't anything he could help. I needed to look it up as quick as possible, because I wanted to understand him and what he was struggling with.

"You're really gone on him, aren't you?"

I snorted. "No."

"Ha. You are."

"Says the one who has to bribe Chloe, because he's too wimp to talk to the bloke he's got a crush on." I might've admitted to having on a crush, but it was actually quite satisfying to have something over Silver for once.

He was the one people liked, who got out and socialised, and who usually didn't have a problem going after what he wanted.

I didn't know why he couldn't just talk to the bloke though. Silver was confident, good-looking, and he had both blokes and girls falling all over for him.

I wasn't jealous of him or anything like that, because I definitely didn't want the attention he tended to get, but I did wish I could be as comfortable in my body as he was in his.

Silver groaned and dropped his head back again. "I am pathetic."

"I'm really not a person to judge. Whatever works for you."

I rose from the sofa and went to get my laptop from my desk. I curled back up in the two-seater with it, and finally opened it. It took a couple of minutes to start up, but once it had I got online and typed in the first link.

Silver watched me out of the corner of his eye. "You really are invested in this, aren't you?"

"It's only been a few days, but I like him. Today was good. We had a good time. He might have issues, but he's also very kind and compassionate and sweet." The website loaded and I clicked on the link that said *about borderline personality disorder*. "It's not about, you know, *sex*. I still don't want it. But I guess kissing is nice and I like being around him."

"Still asexual, huh?"

"Why do you sound disappointed?"

"Because sex is great! How many times do I have to explain that to you?"

"Explain it all you want. It's not going to matter one way or another." I skimmed over the first paragraph, which explained that it was a mental illness marked by unstable moods, behaviour and relationships.

Well, I didn't know about his relationships, but his mood and behaviour were certainly unstable. Sad and depressed one moment, then seemingly happy in the next.

Silver was silent after that. He turned the telly on and switched through the channels.

I continued to read up on the links his brother had provided me with.

An incessant knocking on the door broke the comfortable silence.

Silver rolled his head towards me. "Feel like dealing with that?"

I put my laptop down and got up to open the door.

I stepped back in surprise as Josh fell into my arms. He must've been leaning on it, and I caught him up, keeping him standing. He had a hood drawn over his head and he pressed his face against my collarbone while his hands fisted in my shirt.

The good mood from earlier was gone. This was bad, I could feel it. It was much worse than me saying something wrong, causing him to storm off from the cinema.

I knew it was a lot worse when my hands, which had grabbed onto his arms, came away wet with blood.

"Josh." My breath hitched. He wore a rather thick hooded jumper and the forearms were soaked through with blood.

"You won't leave me, will you?" His voice was muffled, as he still had his face buried against my collarbone.

"No." I hoped that wasn't a promise he would ever remember me making though, because I couldn't tell what would happen in the future.

"She wants to send me away."

"Who does?"

"My mum. She wants to ship me off to Bristol. She wants to be rid of me."

"I'm sure that's not what she meant." Then again, who was I to give advice on mothers? Mine wasn't a role model I could go by. After all, she'd—I shied away from it before I could dig up all the memories I did my best to keep buried. Bringing them back to the forefront wouldn't lead to anything good.

"It was! It is! She doesn't want me around

anymore. She loves her career and I'm too much of a liability!" He was crying now, I could tell from the way he sniffled and his voice had changed octaves.

I put my hands on his upper arms, hoping he hadn't cut so far up. The fabric wasn't heavy with blood there though, so I squeezed a bit, hoping it was comforting. "Maybe getting away from here for a bit would be good for you?"

I realised I'd said the wrong thing when he pushed away from me. His face was mostly in shadow, as he had the hood drawn down over his eyes, but I saw the tears and something dark smudged on his chin. *Blood*.

"You want me gone too. You don't want me!" He backed away, out into the hallway again.

My mind reeled from the sudden shift in mood. "No, that's not—"

"Liar!" A sob rocked his body. "You're such a liar!" And just like at the cinema, he bolted.

I stood frozen.

Heard the main door slam closed.

"Go after him." Silver pushed me and I stumbled out into the hallway, knocking my toe on the threshold. "Go the fuck after him!"

I turned away and ran down the hall to the door, but once I was out on the sidewalk, Josh was gone. I looked both ways frantically, but I couldn't see him. "Shit, shit, shit, shit." I ran back in and bolted into my bedroom to find my phone and his letter.

I still hadn't saved his number on it, so I dialled it furiously as I checked the letter to make sure I pressed in the right numbers. It rang and rang but he didn't answer. Either he'd left it at home, or he was ignoring it.

I tried again, with the same result.

"Fuck!" I felt a sudden need to throw the phone into the wall, but if I broke it I was never going to get a hold of him.

I walked back into the living room, dejected.

Silver had closed the front door and he now leant against it.

"What was that?" I asked him. "What the hell was that?"

Silver shook his head. "I don't know, D. But it was messed up."

I ran my hands through my hair, frustrated.

"D, you've got blood on your hands."

I held them out in front of me where I could see some spots were left. The rest of the blood was on my phone and in my hair. I started scrubbing at my hair, even though I knew it wouldn't do any good. "I don't think I can do this."

"Hey." Silver strode up in front of me. "You can't

give up now. You just said you were invested in him. That you liked him. And he needs help."

"He left, Silver. We're in the middle of London! He could've gone anywhere. It's impossible to find him." How could such a good day turn into a nightmare in the blink of a moment?

"We have to try. I'll help too. We can go opposite ways. Try ringing him again. Do it often. He'll pick up eventually." Silver pushed me towards the door, where we both put on shoes and jackets.

Silver locked the door behind us.

We stood on the pavement, looking both ways.

"I'll go here." Silver pointed right. "You there."

I nodded and headed down the street. I tried Josh's number again, praying for him to pick up. He didn't.

I looked around, hoping to see some sign of him, but I didn't. I tried the number once again—and I was so surprised when someone picked up I nearly dropped my mobile.

"Josh?"

"Who is this?" It wasn't him, but a female. And she sounded weary.

"I—" I took the phone away from my ear to stare at the display. Had I dialled the wrong number anyway? "I'm sorry. I must've dialled wrong. I'm sorry."

"No, wait!" She exclaimed before I could hang up. "This is Joshua's phone."

My heart nearly beat out of my chest. "Where is he?"

"I don't know." Her voice broke on the last syllable. "Who are you?"

Good question. Who was I? A huge fuck-up, that's what. "A friend."

"Do you know where he is? He left." There was such anguish in her voice. This had to be the mother. The one who had wanted to send him away.

"He ran off," I admitted in a whisper. "I don't know where to." I glanced around again. No Josh in sight.

Silence. I knew she was still there though, because I could hear her breathing. "If you find him, will you let me know? I'll keep his phone on me. Just ring or text or something. I need to know he's okay."

"I will," I promised.

"Thank you." And she did sound thankful.

I'd just pressed end call when my phone lit up with an incoming call. "Yeah?"

"Found him," Silver said in the other end.

"Where are you?"

"Soho Square Garden."

I hung up without saying anything else and

started running the opposite way. I passed our flat and continued ahead towards the park.

I saw them once I passed the gates. Silver was standing with his hands in his pockets and Josh was on the ground, head buried in the crook of his elbow. His whole body shook, so I knew he was crying even before I heard his sobs.

My heart broke a little at the sound.

"Josh." I crouched down next to him. "Josh?" I ran my hand over his back. I could feel every bump in his spine through his thick jumper and it worried me. Not as much as his sobs did though. Because hearing them really did break me. "Josh, come home with me. Please."

He didn't move for several long minutes, but then he straightened up a bit and fell around my neck, crying into my shoulder.

My arms wrapped around him instantly, and that was new. I was usually hesitant when it came to this kind of intimacy. I never hugged anyone.

But this was Josh, the beautiful broken boy I'd found crying only days ago in this very park.

The broken boy who'd somehow caught my attention—and I didn't want to let him go.

CHAPTER 12

DAMIAN

*J*osh was curled up on my bed with a pillow clutched to his chest. He was in my clothes again, and I'd cleaned up his arms and put on fresh gauze. I hoped it would stem the bleeding. If it didn't stop, he'd have to go to the A&E.

For now though, all he wanted was to lie down.

I'd sent off a quick text to his phone so his mother wouldn't be worried anymore. Then I'd made us both hot chocolate.

"Here. You should drink some." I sat both mugs on my nightstand.

He didn't react.

He stared straight ahead, but his eyes were clouded.

He'd checked out again.

"Josh?" I crouched down in front of the bed so I could look at him properly. "Josh?"

I remembered reading about this earlier, before he'd shown up. Dissociation. I hadn't finished reading that paragraph, but maybe it was good for him right now to check out for a bit. It'd been real intense for him and if this was how his brain got any kind of rest... well, then I'd leave him to it for a while.

I took my mug and headed back out into the living room.

Silver wasn't on the sofa where he'd been earlier, so I went over to his open bedroom door and knocked on it.

Silver sat at his desk. "How is he?"

I shrugged. "He's not talking at the moment."

"You want me to call V? This is heavy. He knows how to deal with it better than you and I."

I shook my head. "I don't want to do anything without his permission. I don't want a repeat of what just happened."

"I get that." Silver twinned a pen between his fingers. "You know what's happened to him? It's got to be something real bad, right, for him to be so messed up?"

"I've got no idea. But yeah, it's probably

horrible."

He leant back in his chair and looked up towards the ceiling. "We've experienced some heavy shit too. But we've turned out pretty normal, I'd say, considering."

Normal. That wasn't a word I'd ever heard directed towards myself. "Depends on how you define normal."

He grinned. "Well, *I* turned out pretty normal, at least."

"Yeah, right." But he was right. He was the most normal of us. I was glad that he didn't have psychological damage after what had happened to him, at least not to the extent that I did, or Josh.

I wasn't sure if my aloofness had anything to do with my past or if it was just the way I was. Could be both. I could've turned that way after what had happened.

I blew on the hot beverage and took a tentative sip. It was still too hot. "I should go back in."

Silver smiled sadly. "Take care of him."

"I will." I definitely would. Josh needed it. He needed someone in his corner. I should've never agreed with what his mother had proposed earlier. With the mood swings and black-and-white thinking that came with being borderline, of course he'd think I wanted him gone too. That I'd betray him.

He was in the same position I'd left him in, but his eyes followed my path across the floor now, so I knew he was back in the present.

I put my mug down next to his, then crawled over him and lay down closest to the wall.

He turned around slowly. "Have sex with me," he whispered.

I cut my eyes to him. "No."

He instantly felt betrayed. "Why not? Don't you like me?"

"I do. But I'm not going to let you manipulate me into this. I like you, but I'm not going to have sex with you. I'm not." Both because he wasn't in any state of mind to make such a decision, and because I simply didn't want it.

What I'd said to Silver still counted—it wasn't about sex. Sex was never on my mind. My body might like having him close, but not to the extent that it would be noticeable in certain parts.

I wasn't sure that would ever happen.

He closed his eyes.

I expected more tears, but they didn't come.

Instead he lay there with his eyes closed, clutching my pillow to his chest.

"But you can come closer," I offered, and when his eyes popped open, I held my arm out in invitation.

He looked at it as if it was a foreign object, but then he scooted in close to my side and put his head on my shoulder.

I put the duvets over us and got rid of the pillow now pressed in-between us. He seemed to mould into my side the moment it was gone. His arm slid over my waist, resting there rather comfortably.

"Why don't you like sex?" His voice was only a whisper.

"I don't see the appeal." I curled my arm around his shoulders.

His blond hair was wet against my thin T-shirt, because I'd made him take a shower. Once I'd got the hooded jumper off him, it had become evident that he didn't just have blood on his arms and jaw, but a lot of it smudged on the rest of his face and even in his hair.

"But it's good."

"I hear people say that, but it doesn't mean anything to me. I don't have an interest in it." His shoulders were bony. He was too thin. I found myself wondering how often, and how much, he ate.

"Am I bad for liking it?"

This was not taking a good turn. "No. People who like it are far more superior to those like me who don't. Don't worry about it. I'm the abnormal one, not you."

He shook his head, though it was a bit awkward with his head resting against my shoulder. "You don't understand. I *liked* it. Every time he came into my room, or cornered me in the kitchen or the bathroom or pushed me onto the sofa... my body liked it every time, except from when he was too rough. He liked to hurt me, but the times he was gentle, I *liked* it."

Oh shit. "Who's he?" I dreaded the answer.

"My mum's husband. Ex-husband, now."

"Your father?"

Another awkward shake of his head. "Stepfather. I don't know who my father is."

His arm, which had been resting comfortable across my stomach, now lifted up. He put his hand back down on my stomach and splayed it out, twisting the material of my shirt. "Ten years. At least that's as far as I know. I learned to spell when I was six, and that's when I wrote my first journal entry."

Six years old. And sexually abused by an adult who was supposed to care for him. No wonder he was a mess.

"People say that sex is good. Maybe—" This wasn't my area of expertise at all. "Maybe the body likes the stimulation even if the mind doesn't like the person or the situation."

"That's what Vincent told me, too."

Vincent? "What?"

"My psychiatrist."

We lived in London. Surely there couldn't be such a coincidence?

There must be many psychiatrists out there named Vincent, who took in patients with borderline personality disorder and who wasn't related to my best mate.

Right?

"I've been with loads of people, not just him. I've done it voluntarily and it's always been good. So good. But it was with him too, whenever he wasn't hitting me or just ramming it in without any kind of preparation."

Oh God. I really wasn't comfortable talking about sex. Not even hearing about it. It made my skin crawl —but that might have been because he was talking about his stepfather raping him, too.

"Sounds like you've had too much of it," I said instead. I couldn't give him any kind of advice. I hadn't had sex with anyone, and I had no interest in it either. "Isn't it nice to, I don't know, not have to get naked and intimate with someone?"

"But I'm wanted then. For a little while, they only want *me*. They don't care about my scars or my personality, as long as they can fuck me. I want to be *wanted*."

I closed my eyes for a brief second, trying to gather my thoughts. "This is nice isn't it? Just lying like this?"

"Yeah?" He didn't understand where I was going with it.

"This is intimacy too. Of a more innocent kind, perhaps, but still intimacy. I haven't ever done this with anyone else. Only you."

"Really?" He turned his head so he could look at me. His chin dug into my shoulder, but it was more ticklish than painful. His eyes were still red and sore, but they were dry now.

"Yeah. I don't… like people much."

His eyes widened even more. "But you like me?"

"I do." I finally met his eyes head on. He was so close to me. "It's only been a few days since we met, but I like looking at you, and I like being around you even if your mood swings a lot, and I liked it when you kissed me." I wasn't used to talking about my feelings either, though I was more used to it thanks to therapy than the sex-talk. Something I really didn't want to bring back as a subject.

"I can't help it. My moods. One wrong word and I explode. I don't even know how to explain it, but my mind's like a complete mess of emotions that changes in the blink of an eye. It's exhausting."

I couldn't even imagine what it must be like to be

him. I was pretty much aloof in all things. My mood was relatively stable, keeping to the same wavelength most of the time. To switch back and forth like he did...

Yeah, I could imagine it would be exhausting.

"He only got eight years in prison." Josh put his head back down on my shoulder. His index finger made small circles on my stomach. "At least ten years of abuse, though probably longer, because he's been coming into my room for as long as I can remember... and he only gets *eight* years. He's ruined me and in less than a decade he'll be out on the streets again."

I tightened my arm around him at the sudden need to protect him. He didn't need protection anymore though, at least not from that bastard, but the need was churning inside me anyway.

He did need someone, however, someone he could be close to. And *that* could be me.

"Where was your mother in all of this? When I spoke to her, she sounded real worried."

His finger stuttered to a halt. "My mum? When did you chat with her?"

"Earlier. I tried your phone multiple times and eventually she answered it. She was worried, you know. I texted her to say you're fine and that you'll be staying here for the night."

The circles started up again.

It was actually quite nice, relaxing even.

"She doesn't want me there."

"I think she does."

"She wants to ship me off to Bristol. She hates me."

"I think she just worries. Maybe she doesn't know what to do to make you feel better? I'm sure she didn't mean anything bad by it. She was probably just thinking about what was best for you."

I could be speaking complete bullocks.

I didn't know her, after all.

But she had sounded worried on the phone, and it was hard to fake that, wasn't it?

Josh was silent. I hoped what I was saying was registering.

Minutes ticked by and I was getting sleepy. Having him resting against me was something I wasn't used to, but he was warm and those circles he traced on my stomach were relaxing.

I was dozing off.

"You're right," he said eventually. "This *is* nice."

"Mm. Sure is."

I'd never thought I'd say that, that I'd like cuddling with another person, but I did.

I liked cuddling with him.

CHAPTER 13

JOSH

The next morning Damian took me out to breakfast at the Café he worked at.

For once in my life, I felt rested and I knew it had everything to do with sleeping close to him for the entire night.

Like he'd said, and like I'd agreed to, it truly had been nice.

Nice to be so close to someone without anything else being expected.

Nice to feel calm and collected for a few hours, and to get a proper night's sleep without being plagued by nightmares.

A light-haired bloke set our plates down in front of us. "Enjoy your meal."

He had a northern accent and I remembered him briefly from the other day I'd been in here. "Thanks."

I kept my eyes on my plate, afraid that if I glanced around me, I would fade out again like I had last time. Just because of some random man who had looked a bit like Andrew in profile.

I'd got a club sandwich. It looked good, and it was a lot of food on one plate. I wasn't sure I would be able to finish it, but I would try.

"How long have you worked here?" I looked up at Damian. He was safe to look at. He was someone I liked to look at.

"A little over two years. I got the job the summer I was sixteen."

"So you're eighteen now?" I was falling hard and fast for him and I didn't even know his age. I didn't even know his last name, for that matter.

"I'll be nineteen in January."

I hitched my eyebrows up in surprise. "So will I. When's you birthday?"

"The third. Yours?"

"Twenty-third. Our birthdays are only twenty days apart." I didn't know why it pleased me, but it did.

Damian had already started in on his own sandwich. He seemed to be comfortable, content, calm. I wasn't used to anyone being like that around me. My family walked around on eggshells, afraid to set me off, and they were the only other people I knew.

"Is it weird that I've really started to like you? I mean, we've just met."

He paused in his chewing as his gaze landed on me. "Well, in that case I'm weird too."

My heart literally jumped into my throat. I swallowed and swallowed, trying to be rid of the lump that had stuck. I didn't manage it though, so I settled on smiling at him.

His gaze dropped to my mouth, and he stared for a very long second, until his eyes darted away. He started chewing again.

I was pretty sure I could see a distinct flush on his cheeks.

I bit my lip to keep from smiling wider. If I were to guess his thoughts just then I would likely be right.

Kissing.

I hadn't kissed him since we'd gone to the cinema and that had ended in disaster. I wanted to kiss him again, and judging by his reaction just now, I was sure he wouldn't mind if I did.

"What are you going to do once summer's over?" He wanted to change the subject, and I was happy to let him.

"Retake the last year of A-levels. I know I failed

my exams because I didn't even finish them." I twinned my fingers together, nervous all of a sudden. "I was in a real bad place. So bad I was hospitalised, for the third time in two years."

He took another bite of his sandwich as if it wasn't a big deal.

Or maybe he was trying to hide his real feelings for me.

I couldn't tell.

I couldn't read him.

"I'm in therapy four times a week. Two with my psychiatrist and two in group therapy."

"Group therapy?" That seemed to catch his interest. "How's that working out for you?"

I shrugged. "Okay, I guess. But I prefer to just talk with Vincent. We've got more of a connection."

He nodded his head. "My psychiatrist suggested group therapy for me."

"You're in therapy?"

"Yeah." He shrugged it off like it wasn't that big a deal. "Used to go often, a few years ago, but now I generally make an appointment if I feel I need it."

I bit my lip to keep from asking why he was in therapy. It was personal—and if he wanted to share, he would, in his own time. At least I hoped he would.

"What are you going to do afterwards?" he asked.

"Don't know. I should go home. The family's leaving tomorrow and they've been here for me, so I should say goodbye to them." He was starting work once we'd finished eating, so it wasn't like I could spend the day with him.

"How many family members are here?"

"Six. Grandma, my aunt and uncle, and their three kids."

"Wow. That's a handful."

"Mmm. They are. I mean, I love them and all, but they're too much at times. Especially my cousins. Though I should apologise to Cooper for just leaving him at the club." I felt bad about that. Mum had said he'd been looking for me, so he must've been worried. "I guess I should stay home tonight." I didn't want to though.

"We can see each other tomorrow," he said, apparently oblivious to just how much I didn't want to spend the night at home. "I've got the early shift tomorrow, so we can meet up after?"

"Yeah, that sounds good." As long as I got to spend time with him, I'd be happy. I wished he wouldn't even have to work, so we could spend more time together.

"You should eat." He motioned towards my untouched sandwich.

It was delicious, once I finally took a bite.

He glanced over my shoulder, upwards at something.

I turned in my seat to see what he was looking at.

It was a clock.

"My shift's starting. Want to come in back with me while I change?"

I nodded, eager, and took my plate with me.

He carried his own into the kitchen, as he'd already finished his own food.

I sat down on the sofa and continued to chew small pieces at a time while he went to the small row of lockers. He took a black shirt out from the locker, as well as a black apron. He already had on black trousers.

"Are you planning on working here once school starts?"

"Yeah. But not as much as I used to. When I was in college, I worked most evenings, but I doubt I'll be able to do that once I start medical school. It's going to be tough." He pulled off his jumper and it caused the vest he was wearing underneath to hitch up so I could freely ogle the pale, bare skin over the hem of his trousers. Once the jumper was off and his arms dropped back down, so did the vest, hiding his skin from view again.

"What's your flatmate going to do? Is he going to medical school too?"

That caused him to chuckle. "Silver's apprenticing with a tattoo artist. College was more than enough school for him. He's doing what he's always wanted to do, and he's happy with it."

"That's nice. To know what he wants to do. You too." I wasn't sure I would ever be able to do anything. Who would hire a mentally unstable person, after all?

"You'll figure it out. If you have to retake your A-levels, you still have another year to go." He cast me a small smile over his shoulder. He was buttoning up his shirt now, and he did it all up before he turned back to face me.

"I hope so." I finished the sandwich. Seemed I had it in me after all, to actually finish all the food on my plate. "I have to come eat here more often. This was good."

Another small smile as he tied his apron around his hips. "I have to go. My shift has started."

I stood up, anxiety coursing through me all of a sudden. "Tomorrow, right? We'll see each other again then?" I didn't want our paths to split up, not even for a little while.

"Yeah. Tomorrow." His gaze rested on me and we stood facing each other like that, the silence stretching between us.

I wanted to kiss him. He'd said last night that

he'd liked it when I kissed him…

But as I took a step forward, the door opened, and the light-haired bloke with the northern accent stepped into the room.

"Oh. Hey." He smiled at us.

"See you tomorrow." Damian cast me one last fleeting glance, then brushed past his co-worker.

I stared after him, dejected.

"I'm Leslie." He offered his hand.

I blinked at it, then realised he was introducing himself, so I shook it. "Hey. I'm Josh."

"Nice to meet you, Josh." He had a sweet smile, one that was friendly without any kind of judgement.

"You too." I was so bad at small talk. What more was I supposed to say? What had I said to Damian? Not a whole lot. But then he'd approached me when I was utterly depressed, and he'd taken me in and fixed me up.

"So you're a friend of Damian's, huh?" He ventured over to his locker and started unbuttoning the black shirt that was a replica of the one Damian had just changed into.

"Yeah. You worked together long?"

"Almost two years. He started a little while before I did. Don't really know him though." He flashed me a grin.

"You've worked together two years and you don't

know him?" That was kind of hard to comprehend.

"He's not exactly the kind of person who's open to new acquaintances. Spencer, our third co-worker, doesn't know him either. He's not interested in socialising with us."

He'd just finished talking when another bloke walked into the room. This one was brown-haired and wore glasses.

He also seemed to only have eyes for Leslie. "You ready to head out?"

"Just a sec." Leslie took off the shirt and put on a hooded jumper. "This is Josh. He's a friend of Damian's. Josh, this is Spencer."

The last co-worker. I shook hands with him, and he too had a friendly smile.

I liked them.

"I didn't know Damian had any friends outside of that big, fit, tattooed bloke."

"Fit?" Leslie jabbed an elbow into Spencer's side. "You think he's fit?"

"Well, he is." Spencer's hand settled around Leslie's waist, and that was the moment I realised they were together. They seemed to be comfortable around each other, like they'd been together a long time and knew each other well. "You've said it too, so you can't come here and abuse me for it."

Leslie laughed. "All right, he's fit. Do you agree?"

The last question was directed at me.

"Uh." I was flustered. They were talking about Damian's best mate. I knew he was kind and a good friend, but I hadn't given his looks any thought. I'd only had eyes for Damian since I met him. "I guess." I couldn't disagree with them, because Silver wasn't ugly. Not by a long shot. It was just that Damian was more my type.

They both smiled at me again as they moved towards the door.

"Nice to meet you," Spencer said.

"See you around." Leslie gave me a little wave.

I stood for a moment, just taking in the kindness and the sweetness of the two of them. They'd seemed so normal and so happy. I wished I could look like that sometime.

But that was too much to hope for.

At times I had hopes to be happy. Like today, with Damian.

I could dream and I could hope.

But I knew it would turn around. That the hope wouldn't last.

Because that's what it was like to be me.

A big old mess of emotions.

But Damian liked me.

That brightened up my day.

I just hoped it would last.

CHAPTER 14

JOSH

They were all home and gathered in the living room.

I took a tentative step inside, my eyes darting from one to the other.

Mum stood up and came rushing towards me. "Come with me for a bit." She led me out of the living room and into my bedroom.

I sat down on the edge of my bed, nervous for what was coming next. Yesterday hadn't ended well when we'd talked.

She took my desk chair and wheeled it over so she could sit directly in front of me. Her eyes were big and sad. "Joshua. I'm sorry. Yesterday… I didn't tell you clearly."

"Tell me what?"

"Just how much I love you." She reached out, palms cupping my face and her thumbs stroking my cheekbones. "I never showed you when you were little and I regret that so much. But I'm making up for it now. Or at least I'm trying to. I didn't mean to make it sound like I didn't want you here yesterday, because I do. I don't ever want you to leave me, Joshua. But I thought it would be best for you if you went with them, at least until college starts up. I just thought you'd like to get away. I'm sorry if I was mistaken in that."

I'd let my eyes fall closed while she spoke, because her hands on my face, her obvious affection, felt good.

When she finished, however, I opened them and looked straight into hers. "I want to stay here." I couldn't leave the city now, not when I'd just met Damian.

She nodded jerkily. "Then that's what you'll do. That's what I want too, you know that right? But if you wanted something different, I would've dealt with it."

"I like staying with Damian." It came out a whisper.

She frowned in confusion for a moment before her expression brightened. "The boy from last night?"

"Yeah."

"When'd you meet him? Last time I checked you didn't have any fr—" She cut herself off from finishing that sentence, probably afraid I'd lose it again.

"It's okay. You can say it. I *don't* have any friends." That was easy to admit—not so easy to do anything about. "He's my friend though. I *really* like him."

Her eyes searched my face as her eyebrows drew together again. She understood I liked him more than a friend, and she wasn't sure what to feel about it. "Be careful, Joshua. I don't want you to get hurt again, in any kind of way."

"You know that's going to happen, Mum. Even if he means to or not. I can't be trusted. You know that."

"That's not true." Her grip on my face tightened. "You have difficulty controlling your emotions. That's not the same as you can't be trusted."

"But I can't," I argued. "It's not just my emotions. It's the impulsivity and all of the other symptoms too. I can't trust myself, so how can someone else ever trust me?"

She pressed her lips into a thin line. "I love you no matter what. I hope you know that."

I nodded.

I knew it now, when she said it.

"We're all going out to eat tonight, to say good-bye. They leave early tomorrow. Grandma will stay here for a while longer, though."

"I know." The rest of the family had jobs and school to get back to, but Grandma didn't have anything. She'd been a housewife all her life, and once her husband had died, long before I was born, she'd been living off her immense trust fund. Grandma was so rich she wouldn't have to lift a finger for the rest of her life.

It was a surreal thought.

Mum was rich too, but she didn't show it. She went to work and lived off the money she earned. And her trust fund stayed safely in the bank.

So did mine, for that sake.

Though I may have to become like Grandma if I never got well enough to hold down a job.

"Will you come to dinner with us? They'd all like it very much if you did."

"Yeah. Okay." I managed a small, tight smile. "But until we leave, I think I'll just stay here."

Mum seemed to understand. She leaned forward to kiss my forehead, then let her hands fall away from my face. "I'll come get you when we're ready to leave."

She closed the door after her when she left.

I fell back down on the bed and rubbed my hands over my face. Dinner would be nice, I reckoned, and then tomorrow they'd leave and everything would be calm and quiet again.

A soft knock sounded on the door.

"Yeah?" I pushed up on my elbows so I could see who it was.

"Hey, can I come in for a bit?" It was Cooper.

"Yeah, sure."

He came inside and sat down on the desk chair Mum had just vacated. He took me in, from head to toe.

"I'm sorry about the other night. I should've watched out for you more."

"It's okay, Coop. Really." I'd ended up with Damian, so I wasn't complaining at all.

"You sure?" He actually seemed pretty torn about it.

"Yeah. My night ended—well, not fantastic, considering I was smashed, but the next morning was pretty good."

A slow smile spread on Cooper's lips. "You've met someone, haven't you?"

"Maybe." My sudden blush gave me away.

He smiled wider. "Boy or girl?"

"Boy." Obviously. Girls had never been of any interest to me.

"That's great, Josh. I'm happy for you." He leaned back in the chair, getting comfortable. "Is he good?"

"Good? Yeah."

There was a wicked gleam in Cooper's eye. "I meant is he good in *bed*?"

"Oh!" I should've known.

I might've been a bit of a slag before, but Cooper had me beat. He probably had all his siblings beat too, if you put them all together. But Cooper was experienced, and he probably had more of a relationship with his conquests than I'd ever had. I'd usually been dumped right after the shag.

"He doesn't want to… *you know*." I couldn't get myself to say the s-word. "Is that normal?"

Cooper scrunched his nose up. "I've never met a bloke who doesn't want sex. That *is* weird. Sure he's into you as much as you're into him?"

"No. I don't know." My head lolled back and forth on my shoulder. I'd been so sure last night, and this morning, but now that I wasn't in his presence I wasn't anymore. "No. Maybe not."

"Trust me. There's not a single bloke out there who doesn't want a hole to stick their dicks."

"He's never been with anyone else either." Cooper's words weren't exactly reassuring.

Cooper blinked. "Maybe he's shy? Like, mad shy."

"Yeah, maybe."

"Or maybe he's asexual."

"Asexual?"

"I thought that was a myth. I've never met a person who doesn't like sex. I mean, it's *amazing*!"

I lay back down on the bed so I could stare up at the ceiling. "I really like him. So much. It's weird, since we've just met and all, but I feel like we have a connection."

"Now that's rare too."

"What?"

"Love at first sight."

I snorted. "It's not love at first sight, Coop."

"Lust at first sight, then."

I shook my head. "It's not that either. I mean, I wouldn't mind jumping into bed with him, but last night… He pointed out to me how nice it was just to lie in bed, all close and snuggly, without the expectations of sex. It was so amazing. I've never done that with a person before. Before it was all about a bang"—or getting affection through a shag, which never worked—"but this isn't. This is more. This is better."

Cooper stared down at me. "Wow. You're getting all sappy in your old age."

"Old age." I chuckled. "I'm like three months

older than you. I don't think that counts as being old."

"Maybe not." Cooper put his feet up on the bed and leaned back further in the chair. "I'm happy for you though. That you've met someone. Maybe things will get easier, huh?"

"Yeah." I could only hope.

I didn't think it was likely.

Love, or something like it, couldn't fix what was wrong with me.

Nothing could.

AUGUST 9TH

I hate my room.

I don't know why. It's not like I have any bad memories from it.

Once Mum found out, she got a new flat, and everything from my old bedroom was thrown away. All the furniture, all the possessions in my new room are new.

Still, I hate it.

When it's dark out and I'm supposed to be sleeping —I can't sleep, because I hate being in there alone.

It's like I'm a kid again, afraid the door will open and he will come inside.

I know he won't. He's in prison, so he can't get anywhere near me.

Still, I fear it.

I fear the nightmares.

I know they'll come if I fall asleep. They always do.

And they terrify me.

AUGUST 9TH

I cut.

Not my arms this time, because they're already cut up pretty badly.

But I needed to, so I did what I usually do when I can't cut my arms. I start in on my thighs. They don't look half as bad as my arms, but I have scars there too. Lots of them.

I have scars everywhere. But the ones I've done myself are mostly on my arms and legs.

The rest of them... those are the ones I want to forget. Those are the ones I dream about, that wake me up and leave me a terrified mess.

Eight years isn't enough for him.

He did this to me.

He broke me.
I hope he rots.

AUGUST 10TH

I'm going to see him again soon. It's only a couple hours left until he's off from work.

I hope he hasn't changed his mind.

I wouldn't blame him if he had though.

I wonder what he'll say, what he'll think, when he finds out I've cut other places other than on my forearms.

I bet he's going to think it's ugly. That I'm ugly.

Because I am.

AUGUST 10TH

So he realised I'd cut my thighs.

Of course he did. He's good at noticing details. Maybe that's what'll make him a good surgeon? I suppose that has to be a good quality in a surgeon, after all.

He didn't push the issue though. I could tell from the look on his face when he realised it, because he'd put his hand on my thigh and I'd flinched. He hadn't done it to seduce me or anything, like other people would've done. It had only been a sympathetic pat, because I'd shared some more about my life.

He's surprisingly easy to talk to. Even if he isn't sharing anything, I haven't got a problem with it.

Maybe I'm being too trusting. But after two years of intense therapy and hospitalisations I'm getting used to talking about it. Not to mention the trial, where I had to rehash everything, to the last little detail, time and time again.

But anyway. He realised it, and though it surprised him, he backed off.

I'm grateful.

He's seen my arms. He's seen the worst. Yet I'm not ready for him to see my legs.

AUGUST 11TH

He let me stay over last night.

It was nice to sleep with him again. I wasn't so lucky to have a nightmare free night like the last time, but the nightmares weren't so bad this time around. I didn't wake him up with them, anyway.

He's at work now.

I'm staying in his flat until it's time for my therapy session.

I guess I finally have something good to tell Vincent about today. He'll be happy for me, I know he will.

I just hope this'll last.

I'm not so sure it will.

CHAPTER 15

DAMIAN

I left Josh asleep in my bed while I grabbed some clothes and snuck out as quietly as I could.

Usually I didn't mind the early shift at the Café, but we'd stayed up late talking, so waking up had been hell.

I'd just closed my bedroom door and turned to the bathroom when I found myself face-to-face with a stranger.

"Hey," he said.

I blinked, surprised, and managed to mumble a reply. The flat was dark, but not so much so that I couldn't see him, so I took him in.

Black hair, ruffled up by sleep. The tips seemed to be lighter than the rest, but I couldn't see the colour in the dark. He was tiny, small and delicate and frail. Something was smudged around his eyes, and it couldn't be anything but make-up. He wore skin-tight dark jeans and a just as tight shirt.

"Sorry, I got to dash." He passed me with a small smile.

I glanced after him. He bent over to put on his shoes and the tight jeans stretched even more.

I turned away and went into the bathroom before he caught me staring at him. It wasn't like I had an interest in seeing anything, after all.

Though I wondered who he was. Obviously a one-night-stand of Silver's, but I'd thought he had a crush on the green-haired bloke I'd seen at the club.

Silver came out of his bedroom when I was in the kitchen making myself toast for breakfast.

"I met your guest." I turned to look at him.

He blinked. "Guest?"

"One-night-stand?"

"Oh, right." He grinned goofily.

"I thought you had a crush on that green-haired bloke. Chloe's friend." I poured juice in a glass and sat down at the table.

Silver sat down across me. His fingers drummed against the table. "It was him. He dyed his hair."

I was taken aback by that. But then I hadn't seen his face up close at the club. I'd been more preoccupied by the green hair. "Oh. Well, congratulations, I guess?"

"You bet." His grin widened. "I'm seeing him for lunch."

I nodded. "Good." I chewed a piece of toast, mulling over my question. "So you shagged him before you even brought him on a date?"

"Since when are you such a romantic?"

I instantly regretted the question. "I'm not."

"Not everyone falls directly into a relationship. Some of us fall directly into bed and then a relationship hopefully follows."

Relationship. I wasn't sure that was what Josh and I had. We spent time together, but we hadn't kissed or anything since the cinema when he'd stormed off. And we definitely weren't getting naked together.

Silver laughed. "You should see your face!"

"What?" I asked, defensive.

"You looked a bit panicked there, mate." He pointed at me.

"I was just thinking about the definition of a relationship. Aren't your activities last night more along the lines of that definition than Josh and I?"

Silver started shaking his head before I'd even finished. "That's shagging. Not like a relationship at all. It can *be* a part of a relationship, and it obviously will be for me if I can get him to date me, but it doesn't have to be. It isn't for the two of you. It can be, sure, but like I said, it doesn't have to be." He folded his arms over his chest. "What's important is love, respect, and trust."

"Since when did you become such an expert on relationships?" I asked grudgingly.

"Since my first relationship. My first and only." He sighed, sadness washing over him for a moment. "I feel guilty for trying to move on, you know, but it's time. Kian is…" He struggled for words. "Kian is amazing."

"I thought you didn't know him."

"I don't. But I will, hopefully. Doesn't mean he can't already be amazing. He's sweet and he's funny and, I think, a little bit broken like the rest of us."

I raised my eyebrows. "That's a good thing?"

Silver nodded. "People who think everything's all sun and rainbows are annoying. Life can be shit, life can deal you a shitty hand, but life can still be great. People who think like that, now they've experienced things, but they can still enjoy what life has to give."

I chewed on my last piece of toast. "Like you."

Another nod. "Yeah. Like me." There was still a hint of sadness to him. But nothing else could be expected.

A glance at the clock had me moving. "I have to go. I'm opening today."

"See you tonight." Silver didn't move from his chair, just waved lazily as I hurried past him.

"If you see Josh before you leave, tell him I'll bring take-away home."

"Will do."

IT WAS A SLOW MORNING. Tuesday's tended to be that way.

I managed the front alone for two hours, and once Spencer came in, we were two people with little to do. It would pick up once lunch got around, but until then I washed every table and the counter just to have something to do.

I went to check my phone, and saw I'd got a text message from Josh.

Mum wants us to have lunch before group. Can I bring her by the Café?

I stared at it, first wondering why he would even have to ask me that, then realising exactly what it meant. If he brought his mother to the Café, for lunch, I would still be here and I would meet her.

Was I ready to meet his *mum*?

Yeah. Sure.

What else was I supposed to reply? It probably wouldn't be so bad. I'd already spoken to her on the phone, after all.

That didn't stop me from being a nervous wreck for the next hour.

Harriet asked me if I was okay when she came in.

Spencer kept shooting me glances, but he didn't say anything.

And then Josh was there. He looked amazing. Well-rested and seemingly in a good mood, if a bit nervous.

"Hey."

I wasn't at the till, but at the edge of the counter, leading out into the rest of the café. "Hey, you."

"Have you had your break?" His eyes were wide and hopeful.

I shook my head. "No, not yet. I can take it now? I'll just go tell Harriet."

He nodded enthusiastically. "That would be great." His smile died as he bit down on his lower lip. "Uh, also, Grandma tagged along."

Great. Two family members at the same time.

And me, who couldn't do small talk to save my life.

I managed a tight smile. "You can just order. I'll be out soon."

Josh smiled and nodded and darn it… I liked it when he smiled.

I went into the kitchen where Harriet was conversing with the cook. The lunch rush hadn't started yet, so I didn't think it would be a problem for me to take my lunch break now.

Harriet's green eyes slid over to me. "Damian?"

"You mind if I take my break now? There's someone I know out there, and well… yeah." I wasn't sure if I wanted her to deny me or not.

"Sure. Make yourself something to eat if you want." She smiled, always in such a good mood and so friendly.

I was too nervous to eat, so I opted out of it. Instead I inched towards the door, and once I reached it I peered outside. I could see the back of Josh's blond head, and he was accompanied by a woman looking so much like him she couldn't possibly be anyone but his mother. The other woman was older, with white hair, but I would guess she used to be blonde too because she looked like an older, more wrinkled version of her daughter.

These were two of the most important people in Josh's life. And he wanted me to meet them.

Me.

I certainly wouldn't live up to any kind of expectations.

"Aren't you going on your break?" Harriet came up behind me.

"Are you sure it's okay?" I chewed on my lower lip, eyes still gazing at Josh.

"I can say no, but that would be a lie."

Josh turned around in that moment and our eyes met.

I was drawn to him. When he looked at me now, I couldn't possibly back out.

"No, it's okay." I walked over and Josh smiled up at me. "Hey."

"Hey, you," he repeated my earlier greeting back at me, causing me to smile too, a much more genuine one than the one I had given him earlier.

I couldn't get over how beautiful he was when he smiled. His whole face lit up. He should do it more often. A lot more often.

I could feel eyes on me and nervously glanced around.

"This is my mum, Angelina," Josh motioned to the stern-looking blonde woman. "And my grandmother, Emily. Mum, grandma, this is Damian. "

"Hey." I shook both their hands.

They mimicked my greeting.

I took the seat next to Josh and now threw a

nervous glance his way. I had no idea what else to say.

He seemed a bit lost too.

A hand touched my sleeve and I instinctually flinched just a little bit.

Josh's mum looked at me. "Thank you, Damian. For the other night."

I nodded. "No problem."

Spencer came with their lunch before anyone could say anything else. He put each plate down in front of them. "Enjoy your food." He turned his head to Josh. "Hi."

"Hey, Spencer."

Spencer walked off.

I glanced from his back to Josh in question.

"I met him on Saturday," Josh said. "He and Leslie. They're cute together."

"What?"

He stared at me. "They're together. You didn't know that?"

I shook my head slowly. Spencer and Leslie, together? I'd never seen evidence of that. Not that I looked at them much or took notice of their behaviour.

"They are, you know." He seemed to be more amused than anything.

"I'll take your word for it." I, on the other hand,

was a bit embarrassed.

Josh chuckled. "I've met them once. You've worked with them for, what was it, two years? And you never realised?"

I shook my head again. "They're not my friends."

A smile spread on his lips. He bowed his head with another chuckle.

I'm glad he was amused, even if it was because of me. Whatever made him smile.

"So, Damian, do you have any family?" It was Josh's grandma—Emily?—who spoke.

"Aunt and uncle, two younger cousins and my aunt's sister, though she's not actually blood related." I hadn't spoken to Chloe since we'd gone to that club. Silver must've been effective in bribing her, seeing as he'd managed to get Kian home with him.

"No parents?" She asked, surprised.

"No." It was a short, curt answer, but I didn't want to talk about my parents. Not even in passing.

She seemed to understand.

She backed off, anyway.

"Damian's starting medical school soon," Josh said, changing the subject.

I hoped he understood my gratitude from the lingering look I gave him.

"Which one?" Josh's mother, Angelina, asked.

"UCL."

She nodded to herself. "Impressive. You must've had good grades to get into it. It's a good programme."

"Top grades all over," I murmured, hating to admit it since it might sound like I was bragging.

I wasn't, not at all. It was just a state of fact.

I was great at school.

Not so much at anything else. Especially anything that required being sociable.

I would try though. Because these two women were Josh's family and, even if we had only just met, Josh was important to me.

CHAPTER 16

JOSH

*O*nce again I was early for group, and once again only Mal was there.

"Hey, Mal." I sat down next to him, like I had last week.

"Hey," he muttered. He seemed to be in a better mood today. He wasn't hunched over, hiding his face or had his arms in his big hooded jumper, anyway.

"How are you?"

He shrugged. "Like usual."

I knew what he meant by that. Upside to having the same diagnosis was I could understand what he went through too. Mind and emotions a mess, every single minute of every single day.

Lunch had been good though.

My mood had stayed rather upbeat through it.

It had been awkward introducing Damian to my mum and Grandma, but at least it was done now. Out in the open. And he'd done it. He'd met them, which had to mean something.

Something good, for us.

"You seem to be in high spirits."

I turned to face him.

That was the most I'd ever heard him say outside of when he spoke in group, and that wasn't very often compared to the rest of us.

"I've met someone." I hadn't shared it in group last week, because then we'd just met and everything had been rocky. But now… things were *good*. I could share it now, both with Mal and with the rest of them. "He's wonderful."

Mal's lips hitched up into a small, sad smile. He turned his head down so I couldn't see his face anymore. "You're lucky. You deserve it."

"I don't know about that." Deserving or non-deserving… I hadn't done anything worth getting as lucky as I'd been by meeting him.

But I was going to take what I'd get.

"You're lucky you *can*," he elaborated.

I frowned.

Out of everyone in group, Mal had the worst story.

I was on a good number two. Ten years of abuse

and a severe mental illness because of it justified that place.

But Mal... His story was so much worse than mine. It hadn't been his stepfather who'd abused him. It had been his mother and his brother... and no one had done anything until it had been too late, until he'd been so beaten and broken it was impossible to rise up from it, to heal from it.

I hadn't seen the extent of Mal's cutting, but I knew he took it further than me. I knew he didn't just cut his arms and thighs, but that his entire chest was subjected to a razor, as well as everything else on his body he could reach.

At least that was what he'd shared with us in group. There wasn't any reason to doubt it.

Part of me was fascinated, so fascinated I wanted to see how Mal looked underneath those clothes, how much more damage he'd done to himself than I had.

The other part was horrified.

But the part that liked the scars was bigger, admired them even. Blood was fascinating.

The other part, the one that was horrified and ashamed, didn't emerge until the first part had done its job properly.

"It's a trial and error, I guess." There wasn't any

guessing about it. One wrong word and my mood would flip to the exact opposite.

I knew it, Damian probably knew it.

Maybe he was just being nice to me to keep me from flipping out again?

But, no.

I didn't think so.

Both Mum and Grandma had told me, after we left the Café, they'd liked him and he seemed like a good bloke. They were good at reading people. They understood other people in a way I would never be able to. They'd said he seemed to like me a lot.

And if he said it and they said it, then it had to be true, right?

The rest of the members of the group started filtering in, which made Mal clamp down. I wasn't particularly interested in talking anymore either.

I WENT HOME AFTER GROUP.

Mum was at work, but Grandma was there.

"Hey, love," she said once she realised I was hovering in the doorway into the kitchen. She'd been puttering around, cleaning and putting everything from the dishwasher away. "Are you hungry? I can make you something?"

"We only had lunch a little while ago," I pointed out.

"True. But you can never eat too much." She smiled.

I tried to mimic it, but I couldn't. My mood had plummeted fast after lunch.

"Are you feeling all right?" She must've seen my struggle.

"I think I'm going to go have a nap." I motioned my head towards the general direction of my bedroom.

"Okay, love. I'll be here if you need anything."

"Thanks, Grandma." I shuffled to my room and all but fell down on my bed.

My whole body felt weighted down. I hated this feeling. This empty, yet so very heavy, feeling of *nothing*. I couldn't even describe it.

I tucked my duvet over me and curled up under it. I wanted to sleep. Sleep was good. When I slept there was no commitment to anything, no feelings. Unless the nightmares came. Then sleeping could be the worst thing there ever was. I hated reliving my nightmares.

I really hoped that for once I would just fall into the darkness, be consumed by it, and wake up feeling refreshed. That was what I always hoped for, but it rarely happened. If only it could happen now...

I groaned in pain as I was shoved to the floor, but I quickly opened my eyes to stare up at the man towering over me. I quivered in fear.

"Joshua," Andrew drawled, gazing down at me with dazed eyes. Lust or sadism, I couldn't decide. I couldn't even decide which one I hoped for, which one would hurt me less. His lust was evident in other parts of his anatomy too, but he got off on causing me pain just as much as he did fucking me.

I trembled violently as he reached down to grab me. He pulled me to my feet. I tried stepping back, away from him, but he grabbed me again and started ripping my shirt up.

Tears fell from my eyes, but I stood there quietly as he undressed me. It would be over quicker if I just let him do what he wanted to do. If I didn't fight back, he might not even hurt me as much.

Big hands grabbed at my skin and threw me down on the bed. "Good boy, Joshua," he muttered. "You're such a good boy."

I shot up in bed, eyes wide and tears streaming. "No, no, no." I sobbed as I untangled myself from the moist duvet and stumbled my way through the room and into the bathroom. I had an adjoining one and for that I was grateful.

I turned the shower on with trembling hands and

I couldn't even muster the strength to take my clothes off before I stepped inside. I sat down in the corner and drew my knees up against my chest. I rested my forehead against my kneecaps and just let the hot water pelt down over me, soaking me all the way through.

I didn't care that I was wearing clothes, that they were getting drenched. I didn't even feel the water.

The dream, the bloody memory, was still playing in my head, on fucking repeat.

It had been over two years now.

Two years since the last time he touched me.

Why couldn't it ever stop?

Why did I have to relive everything every time I fell asleep? It wasn't fair.

I didn't know how long I sat there. Could've been minutes, could've been hours. But when I finally calmed down enough to at least be aware of my surroundings, I turned the water off and stripped out of my clothes inside the stall.

The air was chilly once I stepped out and I found a big, fluffy towel to wrap myself up in. I sat down on the toilet and stared down at my arms for ages. I had discarded the old gauze inside the shower, so I could see all the scars and all the cuts struggling to heal up after my last bout of cutting.

I wanted to cut again.

The urge was so strong but I couldn't find the strength to get up.

I wanted to cut.

I wanted to resist.

I wanted to forget.

I wanted Damian.

He made everything a tiny bit easier to bear.

I did find my strength and I walked out into my bedroom. The towel was discarded somewhere on the way and I put on clean boxers and socks, then found a pair of loose-fitting jeans, a tight vest, and a loose shirt.

I found a bag in my closet and I stuffed a couple of changes of clothes into it. I had the toiletries I needed at his flat, since he'd bought everything for me after the first night. I grabbed my journal from the drawer in my bedside table and stuffed that into the bag too.

After a brief hesitation—at least I *did* hesitate—I also put my razor in the bag. I couldn't resist. I might *need* it.

"Joshua?" Grandma stuck her head out from the living room once I was putting on my outerwear. "Are you leaving?" She eyed the bag that rested at my feet.

"Yeah. Don't expect me home." I couldn't stay.

Whenever I slept in my own bed, the nightmares consumed me.

I couldn't let that happen.

I took out my mobile phone to check the time. Damian would be done at work soon. We could head back to his flat together if I hurried up.

I HAD BEEN in too much of a hurry and arrived at the Café before he was done.

I stood outside, unsure of my decision now that I was there.

What if I was too pushy?

What if he didn't appreciate me showing up once again?

What if he had plans?

"Hey, Josh."

I whirled around. I was surprised—shocked even —that someone spoke my name. I immediately went into defence mode.

But it was only Leslie, Damian's co-worker, the one with the light hair and the northern accent.

"Oh. Hey." My heart beat a mile a minute. I had to calm myself down before it beat out of my chest.

Or before I had a reaction that would prove to the

world once and for all that I was mad and belonged in a mental hospital.

"You waiting for Damian?" He didn't seem to notice my erratic behaviour.

I was still raw from the memories, from not having cut. I couldn't take much.

Apparently not even a conversation.

So I just nodded.

"My shift starts when his ends."

My heart calmed a little. My palms were sweating though, so I wiped them off on my jeans. "Do you like working here?"

"I do. I'd rather be in the kitchen, but I need an education for that." He grinned wryly. "I'm starting culinary school though, so it'll happen soon."

"That's great." Really, it was. I was in awe of everyone who knew what they wanted to do with their life. I didn't have a clue.

Not even a single, little blink of one.

"What are you going to do now?"

"School," I replied vaguely.

"You're not done with A-levels yet?" He seemed to be sympathetic.

"No. One year left." I refrained from mentioning that I should've been had I not failed them the first time around.

"It's only one year, then you can do whatever you want." He smiled and headed inside.

I leaned against the wall next to the windows.

One year.

Right.

As if I had any idea what I would be doing after that year.

Try to keep myself together, more than likely.

Try to keep myself out of hospitalisation.

No wait, that was something I was trying to do now as well.

Try to keep my relationship with Damian intact. If we even had a relationship. I wasn't sure how it worked, exactly. I'd never been in one before.

"Josh!"

My head snapped to the side.

Damian stood there, eyebrows drawn into a frown.

"Hey."

"Hey." He kept frowning at me.

"What?"

"You were checked out. I tried saying your name several times."

"Oh." I turned my head away so he wouldn't see my complete humiliation. I hated when that happened, when I was so deep in my thoughts time just flew past and people couldn't get through to me.

"Hey, come on. I was going to get us take-away. You like curry?"

His frown had smoothed out.

Maybe he didn't mind my dissociation? That's what Vincent called it, anyway.

"I do. Curry's great." We started down the road, side by side, but not touching. I wanted to keep us talking, say something that wouldn't be completely lame. "Silver had fun last night." It was all I could think of.

"What'd you mean?"

"Well, with his sleep-over."

He looked at me. "He told you about it?"

"Eh, no." I had to chuckle, even if I was embarrassed. "I woke up last night, so I went to the bathroom. And I heard them."

It took a couple of seconds for it to dawn on him, but when it did a heavy blush came over his cheeks.

I couldn't help but smile. No matter what had happened to him in the past, there was a certain subject he was so very innocent on. One I was thoroughly *not* innocent in, one I was very familiar with.

But with him it wasn't on the table. And, for now at least, I didn't even mind it. I would go so far as to say I was grateful for it.

AUGUST 12TH

Is this what it feels like to fall in love?

I've never been in love before, so I don't know. But whatever it is, I like what I'm feeling now. I'm only feeling it with him, so it has to be, right?

He seems to be feeling the same. He even kind of said it, didn't he? But I can't help but worry.

Broken, ugly, good-for-nothing me... Whatever would he want me for? He could have anyone with looks like his. So why me? There isn't anything special about me.

Unless special means a particular skill in freaking out about every single thing. There's nothing attractive in that.

Yet he still wants me around.

I must be doing something right.

AUGUST 14TH

Mal wasn't in group today.

Doc told us he'd tried to kill himself—so he'd been hospitalised. The only person there I'd wanted to talk to, and now he wasn't there anymore.

I don't know how long he'll be gone.

Doc didn't either. I asked.

Mal understood. I understood him. We had a connection. I know it. And now he's just gone. Shipped off to some hospital somewhere. Closed up, where I can't even see him.

Not that I could. I'm not family. We're not supposed to have relations outside of group. Keeps everything nice and on the surface and all that.

It's bollocks.

Mal could be my friend. I could've had a friend in him.

I hope he comes back.

If Mal can't make it, what chance have I got?

CHAPTER 17

DAMIAN

"*D*!" I groaned as my shoulder was shaken. It felt like I'd just gone to sleep, so why was I being forcefully woken up already? It was clearly dark, so it was still night. I was supposed to sleep at night, not be awoken.

"D, come on. Damian! It's Josh."

My eyes shot up at that and I pushed myself up on my elbows.

Silver was crouched down in front of the bed and though the room was dark and I couldn't see him, I knew it was him. It couldn't be anyone else.

"Josh?" I felt the bed next to me. It was empty—and cold. Josh must've been up for a while. "What's wrong?"

"He's in the bathroom. Come on, mate. I'm not sure what to do."

I was out of the bed in seconds.

Silver stepped back, letting me pass him as I hurried into the bathroom.

Josh was curled up on the floor next to the bathtub. His sleeve was rolled up, baring his forearm. I could see the blood trickling over the scarred skin. Then I zeroed in on the razor clutched in a shaking, blood-stained hand.

Josh looked up, his green eyes shining with tears. "I'm sorry," he sobbed. "I'm so sorry!"

"Hey. Shhh." I crouched down beside him and slid one arm around his shaking shoulders. The other I put on his hand, gently prying the razor from his bloody fingers. "You don't have to apologise, Josh."

He rocked back and forth. I pulled him close to me and his face came to rest against my collarbone, while his tears wet my T-shirt.

"Is there anything I can do?" Silver stood just inside the door, hesitant and uncertain.

"Get me bandages, clean cloths, and some antiseptic, please?"

He nodded and started going through the cabinets. He deposited it at my side and crouched down next to us. He had even wet one of the cloths and now he held it out to me.

I pressed it gently against Josh's bleeding fore-arm. It sucked up most of the blood, but the minute I moved it away, the blood trickled again.

Josh still sobbed against me, though he had quieted down a bit.

"Here, let me help." Silver put antiseptic on one of the dry cloths, and together we managed to get Josh's arm cleaned up and bandaged properly.

"Did you cut your other arm too?" I gingerly felt under the sleeve of his shirt, but there was no blood. The scarred skin was rough under my touch, reminding me that there was no smooth skin left on either of his arms, only rough scars.

"I'm sorry," Josh whispered brokenly.

I ran my hand through his blond hair, caressing his scalp, while Silver finished by cleaning up Josh's bloody fingers with the wet cloth. He hadn't cut them, thankfully, but they'd been smeared with blood.

"What happened?" I knew what the answer would be, it was always the same, but it was good for Josh to get it out.

"Dreams." Just as expected. "He was—Andrew was—I don't want to remember what he did to me!" The sobs increased again. I held him tighter. "I don't want to remember."

There wasn't anything I could say to that. There

wasn't anything I could do. Forgetting wasn't something that would ever happen, no matter how much Josh wanted to.

I exchanged a look with Silver. He held the bloody cloths.

I glanced down at the razor I'd deposited on the floor once I'd pried it from Josh. I had no idea where he'd got it from, but it hadn't been from our flat. I picked it up and when Silver held out a cloth, I dropped it atop it. Silver threw it all away in the rubbish.

"Do you need more help?" He turned back to look down at us. "Or do you want to be alone?"

"I'm taking him to bed. But thank you. For everything." I hoped he understood just how thankful I was. For waking me, for helping Josh. For everything.

"You don't have to thank me, D." Silver's eyes went to Josh, who was still crying in my arms. "I care about him too, you know. He's important to you. I'll do whatever to make sure he's better."

"I know. But still, thank you." I couldn't have asked for a better best mate.

Silver left the bathroom.

I listened for his bedroom door to close before I looked down at Josh. "Want to come back to bed?"

He nodded jerkily. I helped him stand up, and I kept my arm around his shoulder as we made our way back into my bedroom. I held the duvet up for Josh to crawl under and I slid in after.

Josh instantly rolled over to rest against my side. I wrapped my arm around him again. "I'm sorry I'm such a mess."

"You don't have anything to be sorry for. Cutting has always been your way to deal, so it's not something easily given up. You're going to have setbacks. I know it and I don't blame you."

"How can you even stand to look at me?"

"Josh." I sighed. Hadn't I answered that before? Several times at least. I didn't mind his scars. They were a part of him, they told a history of just how much pain he'd been in. That he was still in.

I did mind that he cut, of course I did, but that was because I cared about him. I knew he couldn't turn a switch to stop it. I knew it took time. I knew he might never find the strength to stop, that he would likely always have setbacks.

I'd read up on it online, so I would know. Knowing made it that much easier for me to understand.

But I didn't judge him for what was wrong with him. Not at all.

"I wish I never knew him. I wish he'd never touched me."

"Josh…" There was a lot I wished for too, like that my mother had never been mentally unstable. Maybe if she hadn't been, she wouldn't have done what she did.

But thinking like that never served any good. Not for me and certainly not for Josh. It only brought him further into the downward spiral that was his constant depression and switching moods.

His hand gripped my side tightly. "I want to go back to sleep. Can you hold me, please? I don't know if I can sleep otherwise."

"Of course."

He rolled over to lie on his side. I mirrored his movements so that I could press up against his back. My arm held him tight.

He relaxed slowly. "Thank you."

I let my eyes fall shut when I'd felt him relax, but now I opened them again. "What for?"

"For talking to me that night. For bringing me home. For putting up with me. For making my bad nights and days so much better. You have no idea how much better you make my life. I know I cut, but I haven't cut so deep I've had to go to A&E in a while now. You're there when I do cut, and you fix me up."

I closed my eyes again. "That's good to hear. That I'm some help, at least."

"You're a lot more than *some* help. A lot more."

I squeezed him tighter. I didn't know what to say, but that wasn't anything out of the ordinary. "We all have scars, Josh. We all have stories to tell." I whispered it against his hair.

His breath caught. "Are you ever going to tell me your story?"

"Someday, maybe." I couldn't bring that shit to the forefront now. School would be starting in less than a month. I didn't have time for a breakdown.

Josh wiggled around a bit until he could comfortably turn his head to look at me. "I won't push for it. I was just curious." His lips were soft when they pressed against mine. There was a salty flavour to them, from his tears earlier.

He didn't push for anything but that chaste kiss either.

I suppose normal blokes would've wanted it to, or expected it to go further than that, but I didn't. I liked the kiss—but that was it. I didn't have a burning need to get naked, hot and heavy. It just wasn't something that would ever happen to me. I'd made my peace with it.

And I thought he appreciated it too. After everything he'd been through, for so long, how could he not?

～

"ARE YOU FEELING BETTER?"

I watched as Josh changed out of the shirt he'd been sleeping in. He always wore thin, long-sleeved shirts to bed. I knew he was embarrassed by his arms, and I didn't push him. It wasn't like I minded him wearing clothes. If he'd slept in less, if he was like Silver and preferred to sleep only in boxers—or in the nude—it would've been a lot more awkward to share a bed with him.

"Yeah." Josh flashed me a smile. He ran his hands down his chest, smoothing the shirt, before he walked over to me. "I'm glad you're not working today. I'm looking forward to spending the day with you."

"Me too." I returned his smile as Josh opened the bedroom door and stepped out into the living room. The smile still on his lips, and the look in his green eyes were more than enough for me to know that I'd done the right thing by saying no to an extra shift.

"Hey, D." Silver's voice came from the front of the room. "You've got visitors."

I turned.

As I didn't know a lot of people, and two of my closest were in the flat with me, there really were only three it could be.

Turned out it was two of them. "Ray. Claire. Hi."

Josh went rigid next to me as he realised whom the two people standing by the door were.

I glanced at him and Josh relaxed again when our eyes met.

"Hi, Damian. We were in the neighbourhood, so we thought we'd stop by and ask you to join us for dinner tonight." Claire smiled widely. She was always in a good mood. "Chloe and Quinn are coming too. You can bring your mate." She nodded toward Josh, who suddenly looked like a deer caught in headlights.

"Uh." I looked to Josh again, catching his eye. I tried to form a silent question and I reckoned I'd succeeded in it, because Josh gave a tiny nod. "Okay. Um, when?" I turned back to face my uncle and aunt. Claire was still smiling, but Ray studied Josh.

"As it's Friday, we're doing dinner a bit later than usual. How about around six?"

I nodded. "Okay. We'll be there."

"Great!" Claire breamed. "See you both then." Her eyes too flickered to Josh, as Ray's had done, before they both left the flat.

They must both be confused. I hadn't told them I

was seeing anyone, so having me come out of my room on a Friday morning with another bloke must be quite a surprise for them both.

"Are you sure about this?" Josh chewed nervously on his lower lip. "Dinner with your family?"

"Yeah. I've met your mum. *And* your grandma. It's only fair that you meet my people." It had only been three days since I met Josh's mum and grandma. Since I'd met them so early—we'd practically only just met ourselves after all—there wasn't anything wrong about him meeting my family.

Maybe we were moving too quickly, but it didn't matter.

I was serious about Josh.

It was time they found out something about my life, too. For so many years, I'd kept myself at a distance to them. I always had, probably always would, but that didn't stop them from loving me. They'd even kept my old bedroom intact, just in case I wanted to come back home and live with them again—or just to stay over a night.

I didn't think they'd mind that Josh was a bloke. I reckoned they'd be happy I'd found someone, no matter the gender. It hadn't exactly been a priority of mine to get out there and date. I knew they worried about me, though they never said so out loud.

I did tend to get lectured by Chloe from time to time, to stop being anti-social and get out to live my life. Maybe I'd even get her off my back now.

That would be a positive thing.

I had grown up with Chloe. She was like a sister to me, with all the good and the bad that entailed. She'd been living with Ray and Claire almost as long as I had.

"As long as you're sure." Josh still chewed on his lower lip.

"I am." I reached out to brush my finger over the small of his back. "I'm sure. It'll be fine. As long as you want to. I'm not going to force you."

His eyes were wide. "I want to, I just—what if they don't like me?"

"Trust me, mate, they'll love you," Silver interjected as he headed into the kitchen. "You are simply adorable."

That brought a sheepish smile to Josh's lips and I reached out to run my fingers in a gentle caress over his cheek. I'd never given a thought to affectionate gestures, but with him they were so easy to make.

At least in private.

"It'll be fine."

Even if it didn't, what did it matter? It wasn't like I saw them that often, and I would still want to be with Josh if they should have some kind of objection against it. They didn't run my life. I ran it very well myself.

I could only hope Silver was right, though, that they would like Josh. And that they wouldn't embarrass me completely.

AUGUST 15TH

He wants me to meet his family.

Shit.

This feels different than when he met mine. So much bigger, somehow.

I don't know why. There's no logic to it.

But shit. What if they don't like me? I want them to. Because I like him. I like him so much.

I don't want this to be what makes or break us.

CHAPTER 18

DAMIAN

*J*osh was asleep with his head on my shoulder.

I didn't mind it, not at all, but it was much easier to relax back in my own flat, in private. Now Ray, Claire, Chloe and her girlfriend were there too, occupying the biggest sofa. Josh and I had the smaller one to ourselves.

Chloe had been shooting me looks I couldn't decipher all evening. She was still doing it, though she too seemed a bit sleepy. She was pressed up against Quinn's side, whose attention was solely focused on the telly.

Claire was resting against Ray, and they seemed comfortable doing it.

I didn't think I looked that comfortable. Not now,

with all of them around me, with Chloe shooting me glances all the time.

I didn't mind having Josh pressed up against me, not at all. It was just a bit weird to have my whatever-he-was—were we boyfriends yet?—over at Ray and Claire's house. The house I'd grown up in. It was weird being in close contact with anyone in front of them, because I'd never been a fan of physical contact before. I couldn't even remember ever hugging one of them.

"So how come you've got a boyfriend?" Chloe finally found her voice. I wasn't sure I was grateful she was getting it out or wishing she'd just stuck to sending me those looks. "You of all people."

"What's that supposed to mean?" I threw a glare her way, but soon cut my eyes back to the telly.

"It wasn't meant to be rude, it's just..." She did a vague motion with her hand. I could see it from the corner of my eye. "You've never been into people. Especially not physical contact with people. You've never shown an interest in *anyone*."

"Things change." I glanced down at Josh.

He slept on. He couldn't have got much sleep last night, with his nightmares and the cutting. He probably hadn't gone back to sleep after we'd got back in bed either.

"You meet the right person." Maybe it was too

quick to say that he was any kind of right person for me, but it did feel right.

"So it's serious between you two?" Chloe studied me curiously now. Like I was an attraction to be gawked at.

"Yeah." It was, wasn't it? I didn't do people, but I somehow did him.

I could share my bed with him without it making me feel sick by the simple thought. I could hug him or hold him or kiss him, and it only made me feel good, not repulsed, like I'd always imagined I'd feel if someone ever got close to me.

Besides, I didn't think I had it in me not to be serious. Maybe I needed to have a deep, emotional connection with someone for it to click, and I'd had that with Josh since that first night we'd met.

Something between us—chemistry, feelings, whatever it was called—had been instantaneous.

I tilted my head to rest against the back of the sofa.

Chloe stretched sleepily and pressed in further against Quinn, who wrapped an arm around her shoulders.

It was dark outside. The clock had to be nearing eleven by now. The film we were watching had started around half past nine. It wasn't exactly my kind of film. But then again, I didn't have a particular type I liked. I hardly ever watched them. I never had time. I studied, I worked, and now I also spent time with Josh. There weren't enough hours in the day for anything else.

My eyes were threatening to fall shut when Josh suddenly jerked away from me with a gasp. The sudden movement upset his balance and he fell to the floor, where his shoulder connected hard with the coffee table. Josh curled up and his hands tore at the bandages around his forearms.

I blinked, disoriented at just what had happened.

Josh had managed to rip up the bandages, and he scratched at his recent cuts, breaking up the fresh scabs.

"Josh." I bent down and grabbed both of his wrists, then wrapped my arms around him so that Josh's hands were pressed up against his own chest. He trembled against me. "It was just a nightmare." I rested my cheek against his. "It's fine. You're fine."

The trembling subsided slowly. He'd been half-asleep when he'd tried to hurt himself, still trapped in whatever nightmare he'd had, but he blinked himself into awareness now.

"Come on." I pulled him up on the sofa.

Josh's eyes were watery when he finally turned to face me.

I turned his arms over to look at where he'd

scratched himself. A few of the scabs had broken and there was some blood, but not a lot. Not like the night before.

"How's your shoulder?" It had taken quite a hit against the table.

"Fine," he murmured as his eyes fell to his lap.

I manoeuvred us around until we were both stretched out on the sofa. Josh was pressed up against the back of the sofa and me, and he settled down resting against my side, his head on my chest. I ran my fingers through his hair, massaging his scalp gently. I'd discovered that it relaxed him more easily. "It's okay. I'm here."

He nodded, but his hands fisted in my shirt and held tight.

I could feel eyes on me. I knew they were all watching me and Josh, that they'd all seen Josh's forearms. I couldn't tell them anything though, because it wasn't my story to tell. So I avoided looking at them. It wasn't like I wanted to tell them, even if I could.

"You should both stay overnight, Damian," Claire said softly. "You're both tired. It wouldn't serve you any good to take the bus home at this hour."

"Yeah. Okay." I stared at Josh's blond head. The strands were soft against my fingers. He never had gel or wax in it. "Is my room fit to stay in?" I hadn't slept in my old bedroom since I'd moved out.

"It always is, Damian. Just in case." I could hear Claire settling down on the sofa again and when I chanced a glance over I saw her leaning against Ray, who had his arms around her.

I met Chloe's eyes when I looked over at her, but she didn't say anything. I didn't either. I focused back on the telly.

Josh fell asleep again, I could tell from the way he relaxed and from the way his breathing evened out.

Josh was troubled. More so than me; at least I thought so. I didn't have the kind of problems Josh had.

I felt I was in over my head with him most of the time, but at the same time I couldn't find it in myself to let him go. It was all so new, but just the simple thought of not having him around anymore made my chest squeeze to the point of physical pain.

And when Josh told me I made it better, then I knew it was all worth it.

～

I LED the way up to the kitchen the next morning.

Josh trailed behind me. I could picture how he

wrung his hands together as he tended to do when he got nervous.

Ray, Claire, Chloe, and Quinn were seated at the table, eating breakfast. I could hear the telly on in the living room, so my younger cousins must be in there. It was just as well. They didn't need to know anything about Josh's problems. They were too young.

I'd already told Josh he didn't have to say anything to them, but he insisted he had to. They'd seen his arms, so it was only fair, was his argument. I wasn't so sure about that, but it was Josh's decisions, so I'd let it go.

"Morning." I pulled out two chairs and sat down on one of them.

Josh was wringing his hands, just as I'd pictured. His eyes flickered around nervously. I didn't know why he insisted it was important to talk about it when it made him so skittish. They didn't *need* to know.

Just because they'd seen his arms didn't entitle them to his story.

"Morning," Josh murmured too as he sank down on the chair next to me I'd pulled out for him.

They all answered the greeting and they all sounded polite while doing so. I saw they were curious though by the way their eyes lingered a little longer on Josh than they should've.

Josh glanced at me and I held his eyes until Josh let his own drop. If he chose not to tell them after all, I would be fine with that. Whatever Josh wanted, I would support.

"About last night—" Josh started hesitantly.

"It's okay." Claire bent forward. "You don't have to tell us anything."

"I want to. You're Damian's family. And you saw… it's important to talk about it." His eyes flickered between them. "You saw my arms." He took a shaking breath. "I've been cutting myself for years. My stepfather, he—" And stop.

"Josh." I could see how agitated he became by the simple mention of his stepfather. Mentioning him, or having anything remind him of Andrew, or the terrible nightmares he had almost every night was what drove Josh over the edge time and time again.

I didn't understand why it was so important to talk about when it always led to him hurting himself.

"You don't have to say it, Josh. We understand." Claire's voice was low.

Josh nodded slightly at her words. His Adam's apple bobbed up and down for every swallow he did as he tried to find his voice again.

"It's okay." Claire reached across the table to pat

his hand. Josh's hand twitched in surprise, but it slowly settled under hers.

I reached under the table to put my own hand on his thigh. I squeezed and Josh cast me a quick, darting glance. I gave him a barely there smile and he returned it.

He had his bad days. Sometimes they were very bad. But he always overcame them and things were good until the next time.

As long as he had those good days in-between all the heavy days, I knew he would be fine.

"So that could've gone better."

Josh collapsed on the sofa with a sigh.

"I think it went fine." I went over to look down at him. "They liked you."

Josh laughed derisively. "I never should've gone with you. I was having a bad day and I knew something would happen. It always does. And it did. They saw just how messed up I am. They're not going to want that for you. To be with someone like me."

"Josh." I sat down on the arm of the sofa. "They don't care about your arms or the state of your mind or whatever else that might be going on with you. All they care about is that you make me happy. They're my family. They trust my judgement. And even if they hadn't, they couldn't have swayed me. It's my life."

His green eyes were wide and insecure. "You really think they liked me?"

"They did." At least I hoped so. I wasn't the best at reading people, but I had paid particular attention to them both last night and this morning. I hadn't seen anything but sincere curiosity directed towards Josh. "How could they not?" I leaned down a bit to brush my fingers over his smooth cheek.

Josh pushed himself up and my fingers slipped down to cup the back of his neck as our lips met in a kiss. Josh's arms wrapped around my waist and he pushed closer. I spread my knees to accommodate him in-between them. This was the first time, since the first night anyway, when he'd been sitting atop me, that we were so close while kissing.

Kissing had never held any appeal to me.

Until I met Josh.

Kissing Josh was amazing, even though I knew I had to be bad at it.

The front door opened and slammed shut.

"How did it go?" Silver asked as he strode past us towards the kitchen.

"Badly," Josh mumbled as he pulled out of the kiss. He rested his head against my chest.

Silver stopped before he reached the threshold and turned around. His eyebrows rose questionably. "Badly?"

"Not that bad." I wrapped my arms around his shoulders. "They liked him."

"That's still in debate," he argued. "Don't know that for certain."

"Did anything happen?" Silver glanced between us.

"You know, just me. Being me. Messed up. Like usual." Josh shrugged, like it wasn't a big deal, but I knew it was.

Silver could obviously tell as well, because he came over to brace his arms on the back of the sofa. "So what if you had a messed up day? That doesn't mean you're not a great person. Because you are, you know."

I tilted my head to the side so I could look at Josh's face. A small smile flitted over his lips.

I directed my own smile at Silver, who in turned winked back at me. I guess Josh had to hear things from someone else sometimes for it to sink in, and Josh did trust Silver.

Silver had been nothing but kind to him. He'd always been trustworthy. I was glad they got along so well.

My family wasn't important. Whether they liked

Josh or not, it wouldn't really have any impact on me. It wasn't like I saw them that often.

Silver and Josh were the two most important people in my life, and as long as they got along, everything would be fine.

AUGUST 16TH

I never should've gone to meet his family. Not after the night I'd had.

Even if he says they liked me, I'm not sure I believe it. I mean, how can they? They saw my arms, saw what I do to myself.

I wouldn't have wanted that for my nephew, if I had one. How could they possibly want it for theirs?

He doesn't seem concerned though.

I guess he must really like me.

AUGUST 17TH

Grandma left today.

I went home to say goodbye. It was hard, even if I'd hardly ever been home while she's been here. She's been here for me, after all, and I haven't even had time for her.

I feel guilty. So bloody guilty.

She hugged me tight and kissed me on the cheek before she left us to head into the pavilion. Grandma doesn't drive, so she has to take the train. Mum and I saw her off.

Mum says that I can go visit her whenever I want. That she'll even come with, if I want her to, and if she can get time off of work.

I love them.

I love them so much.

I hate when they leave.

AUGUST 19TH

College's starting up soon. Damian's starting med-school. Things will change, I know they will. I will have lots to do, and so will he. He'll probably have more, because medical school is so full on.

I think I'm already in love with him. I can't imagine being without him for even a second.

He still hasn't told me anything about himself, which does bother me, but he never shies away from me, and that again pleases me. He's very attentive.

We just fell into this, whatever it is. I don't know if we're boyfriends yet or not. I haven't dared asked, because I'm afraid of the answer.

I should ask.

I know I should.

But it's scary.

What if he says no?

CHAPTER 19

"*H*ey Josh, want to come out with us?"

I turned from my position on Damian's bed to look at Silver standing in the doorway. "Where're you going?"

"Heaven."

Clubbing and alcohol. I was definitely in.

He grinned at me. "I'll text D, so he knows where we are when he's off work. Who knows, maybe he'll join us."

I changed into some finer clothes and tried to sort my hair out. It was getting too long. I should get it cut soon. Before college started, definitely.

"You're looking good!" Kian winked at me once I exited the bathroom.

I looked plain compared to him.

Kian was tiny, with black, spiky hair with multi-coloured tips. He wore tight clothes and make-up, and he had the mannerism and the lilting speech of the stereotype gay that tended to be parodied on the telly.

He was adorable though.

And he fit so well with Silver.

I didn't know why, considering they weren't anything alike. Silver was big, broad, muscled and covered in tattoos. I bet he could break Kian with a single hand. Silver was kind, and could be a laugh, but mostly he was a calm and serious bloke.

Opposites did attract, apparently.

Wasn't that true for my own relationship too? If it even was a relationship. I still hadn't dared bring up the labelling. Maybe I could do it tonight, when I was drunk. Everything was so much easier then.

"You look good too," I told Kian. "Both of you do." It wasn't a lie. Silver had to be one of the most handsome people I'd ever seen—and Kian the prettiest. At least the prettiest bloke I'd ever seen.

"So do you." Silver clapped my shoulder.

Not even an hour later we were in the club and the night was in full swing.

"Shots?" Kian yelled in my ear so as to be heard over the thumping music.

I nodded, and he leaned over the bar to yell something in the barman's ear. The bloke nodded and proceeded to fill not just two, but six shot glasses.

Kian slid three of them over to me. "Show's on." He grinned.

Well, if there was anything I knew, besides sex, it was how to down shots. I hadn't had a drink since that time I went out with Cooper, and I couldn't remember much of that night.

Before that... it'd been a while. I'd been sober through my whole hospitalisation, and then I'd been released right in the middle of the trial.

I downed the shots in quick succession.

So did Kian. "Now that's going to get things started." He slid all shot glasses away from us and then swivelled around so he could see the dance floor.

Silver headed towards us from where he'd been detained at the door by someone he knew. He grinned and grabbed Kian around the waist, swinging him around so that Silver was now leaning back against the bar and Kian was leaning on him.

"Smooth," I heard Kian say before he leaned up and in to kiss Silver passionately.

I couldn't help but watch them.

I'd kissed a lot in my life, but not like that. Not with real passion, passion for a person I cared for.

Kissing had used to be part of getting a shag— and now it was just something chaste with Damian.

Not that I didn't appreciate what we had, because I did, but looking at them now... I wanted to be kissed like that. Like I was something to be devoured, like he couldn't get enough of me.

"Hey, Josh."

I startled around to my other side when someone touched my arm.

"Oh, hey!" My heart calmed down when I recognised Spencer. "You're not working?"

He shook his head, eyes cutting over to the dance-floor. I follow his line of sight and saw Leslie out there, dancing with a gal our age with long, hazel, wavy hair. "We both have the night off, so we're enjoying ourselves."

"Is Damian working alone?" I knew he did sometimes.

"Harriet's closing up with him tonight, I think. She stays late a couple of days a week, either alone or with one of us." Spencer smiled at me. "Damian joining you here after work?"

"I—I don't know." I hadn't asked Silver if he'd got an answer to his text. I couldn't at the moment, either, because he was rather busy. They couldn't keep their hands off each other.

Spencer leaned forward so he could look at Silver and Kian too. "That's Damian's mate, right? The tattooed one?"

"Yeah. That's Silver. And his new boyfriend, Kian." The fact that I was talking to someone else, and had just introduced them, didn't even register with them. "They're a bit… hands on." I smiled sheepishly.

"New love." Spencer grinned. His hazel-brown hair was styled in a messy manner, and he was wearing the black-framed glasses he always wore.

"How long have you and Leslie been together?" It seemed a good subject for conversation, even if we had to lean in close and shout to be heard over the music.

"A year, come October." Spencer's eyes seemed to sparkle behind his glasses. "We danced around each other for a while. How long have you known Damian?"

"About two weeks." That was nothing compared to them.

A year.

I wondered if Damian would want to stay in my life for so long.

Spencer's eyebrows lifted in surprise. "Fourteen *days*?" He didn't get to say anything else, because he suddenly had an armful of styled up brunette in his arms.

"Thirsty." She waved her hand in front of her. "Order me a drink, please?"

Spencer rolled his eyes, but turned around to do as she asked.

She smiled in satisfaction, face turning towards me, and I blinked in surprise. Except for the fact that she was a girl and Spencer a lad, they looked exactly alike.

Twins.

"Josh. Hey." Leslie had followed her off the dance floor and was now standing in front of me.

"Who's this?" Spencer's twin took me in, from top to toe and back up again.

"This is Josh. Friend of Damian's. You know, our co-worker?"

She nodded. "You look fine." That was directed at me.

"T-thanks." I was flustered. No one ever complimented me much. Before I'd only got compliments during sex, but that had either been how good I'd been at sucking them off, or how good I'd been at taking their cocks.

"A shy one." She stroked a hand over my shoulder.

"Steph. Let off him." Leslie was firm. "He's gay."

Her perfectly shaped eyebrows inched up her forehead. "You are?"

I nodded quickly.

She blew out a breath. "That's a darn shame that."

Spencer turned back around with her drink and she fluttered off.

He stared at her, while Leslie stepped even closer to both of us.

"Good thing you are. I wasn't sure, but she can be a bit—" He waved his hand, trying to find the word.

"Of a slag?" Spencer suggested.

"I was trying to find a nicer word for it."

"There isn't a nicer word for it."

Leslie rolled his eyes now. "Anyway. She can be a bit out there, you know? So that's why I said it. I mean, I got this vibe you were with Damian, but I can't know for certain, obviously."

Was that his way of indirectly asking if I was with Damian? Or was he just making an observation? "I am. I'm gay. It's cool."

Silver's hand clamped down on my shoulder, bringing my attention to my other side.

"Want another drink?" He asked me. He had a good grip around Kian's waist, and both their eyes rested on me curiously.

"I'll have whatever you're having." I picked some money up of my pocket. Kian had paid for the shots, but I didn't want them to pay for anything else. I pushed it into Silver's hand so he'd take it, and he nodded as he turned to the bar.

"Who're your friends?" Kian asked me.

Friends? "Oh. This is Leslie and Spencer." I motioned at them in turn. Kian stepped forward to shake both their hands.

"I'm Kian," he introduced himself. "Nice to meet you." Both Leslie and Spencer told him so back. Kian's eyes widened when he heard Leslie speak. "Where are you from, love?"

Leslie smiled. I was sure he got that question a lot. "Newcastle."

"Proper Geordie, huh?"

Leslie laughed. "Starting to turn into a proper Londoner by now."

Silver thrust my drink at me and I sipped at it. It had a bitter taste to it, but it was rather good.

"You okay?" Silver leaned in to speak into my ear.

I nodded. "Did Damian answer your text?"

"He said to have fun."

"Was he going to stop by once he was done?" I asked, hopeful.

Silver shook his head. "Didn't say."

The disappointment was heavy and I took a big sip of the drink. I wasn't sure why I was disappointed in the first place, because going out had never been our plan. I knew he didn't like it. This wasn't his scene.

Still, I wanted to see him.

"Want to dance with me?" Kian was back in front

of Silver and his fingers fisted in the front of Silver's shirt. Silver only grinned, and Kian dragged him out onto the dance floor.

I glanced sideways.

Leslie had stepped in close to Spencer. They said something to each other, something I couldn't hear. They both smiled and shared a kiss.

I didn't want to be there anymore. Everyone was so normal and happy, and there I stood, strange and alone. Why couldn't anyone love me? I just wanted to be loved. I'd take that over anything any day.

Damian might like me, but he wasn't like Silver and Kian, and Spencer and Leslie. He didn't touch me like that or kiss me like that. We were more platonic friends than anything. Friends who shared a bed most nights, because I never went home. We'd only kissed when I'd taken the initiative to it.

I emptied the rest of my drink and turned around to order another one. A drink *and* a shot.

I didn't know how much I drank. I knew I drank a lot, but I didn't keep count on it.

I wandered away from the bar at some point, away from Spencer and Leslie, who seemed so happy together and so very much in love.

Away from the sight of Silver and Kian dancing close, kissing, and practically shagging on the dance floor.

My eyes burned.

I knew I was going to cry.

How could the night have gone from being good to shit? I'd gone out with two blokes I liked, met another two that seemed nice and who I wanted to get to know. And in an instant my mind had gone to shit.

No wonder I didn't have anyone to be with. Who would want to be with someone like me?

He felt sorry for me, that's what it was.

How could he possibly want to be close to me when I was such a bloody mess? And I meant that quite literally too.

A sob escaped me as I stumbled into the toilets.

But I want him.

I wanted to be with him. I hadn't even known him a month yet and I was *so* attached. Was that part of my disorder, like everything else about me? Had I become so attached to him in such a short time because I was borderline, because I was brain damaged?

Another sob escaped and I locked myself in a free stall.

I sank to the floor and buried my face in my hands.

Why can't I just be normal?

CHAPTER 20

*A*ngelina came breezing into the Café as I washed the tables.

Something stuck in me.

I realised it was fear.

She was alone, no Josh trailing after her, like he sometimes did. They had lunch at the Café occasionally, just the two of them, and I even joined if it coincided with my break.

"Hi, Damian." She looked a bit startled at seeing me.

"Hey." I frowned. "Is Josh okay?"

"Josh? Yeah, I reckon. I haven't spoken to him today." She didn't sound or seem concerned. But if she wasn't here because of Josh, then why?

"Angelina." Harriet came out from the back-room, jacket over one arm and a purse in the other.

"Ready?" Josh's mum smiled at her.

My eyes darted between them. Did they know each other?

"I'll see you later, Damian." Angelina cast me a brief smile.

"See you tomorrow." Harriet waved at me.

Then they were out the door and walking past the windows. Together, in what seemed to be amiable conversation.

Harriet had asked me earlier if it was okay for me if she left before we closed. I was used to closing on my own, so I hadn't minded. It wasn't like there were any people here to keep up with, after all. She hadn't mentioned she was leaving with Josh's mum though.

The fear that had taken hold of me when Angelina walked in, slowly dissipated as I continued wiping down the rest of the tables. For a moment I had expected something to be wrong with Josh, and it had *terrified* me.

The last hour seemed to drag by. No one stopped by this late. Harriet had been talking about starting to close earlier, when the kitchen closed, because the next couple of hours just weren't worth it.

The bell rang when there was fifteen minutes left and I sighed heavily before turning around. I did not want to deal with someone in the last fifteen minutes. I just wanted to clean up and go home—

"Josh?"

He stood just inside the door. One hand gripped his opposite elbow and his head was bowed.

It was bad.

I could tell from the stance.

"Hey." I stepped around the counter and went over to him. I locked the door so no one would interrupt us, then put my hands on his shoulders and led him over to a chair so he could sit down.

"What's wrong?" Something must've happened at the club. Silver had texted me to say they were going out.

Josh shook his head. He was crying, even if he was still refusing to look at me.

"Josh." I swallowed a lump that threatened to get stuck in my throat. "Josh?" I ran my hands over his shoulder, over his neck, and up to cup his cheeks. I wiped away tears with both of my thumbs. "Please tell me what's wrong."

He buried his face in his hands. I was still cupping his cheeks, so part of his hands covered mine. It didn't seem like he even noticed.

"If I'd been normal, would we have been normal?"

He mumbled it and for a moment I was sure I

heard him wrong. "What?" Normal? "What are you talking about?"

"Everyone's so happy." He was still mumbling, but I leant closer to him so I could catch everything he said. "Happy with themselves, with each other. They're comfortable with each other. Like, really comfortable. We're not. Not like that."

"Who're they?" I still had no idea what exactly he was on about. What did he mean by normal?

"Spencer and Leslie's been together for a long time, but Silver and Kian met after we did. Yet they're all over each other."

Were we really back to the whole sex issue?

"I'm not the same person they are." I got annoyed. I couldn't help it. Hadn't I been clear about it all?

"What's so wrong with me that we can't be like that?" He started crying harder.

"There's nothing wrong with you." Not when it came to this anyway. But I didn't know how to make him understand.

"Is it my scars? Is it the fact that I'm borderline? That it's bloody brain damage? Do you think I'm less because of it? Is it because of Andrew and what he did to me, because I liked it?"

"Whoa! *Josh*." I gripped his face harder. "No, it's not your scars or your disorder or what your stepfather did to you. Well, maybe sort of the last one, because I think the last thing you need right now is sex—"

"But that's all I know! That's all I am. It's all I'm good at. And I can't give you the one thing I know how to do." More sobbing, more tears.

"I don't want you to," I said, drawing out the words so he'd hopefully get what I was saying to him. "I don't want sex. And that has nothing at all to do with you. I think you're wonderful, Josh. But I don't crave sex like other people. I'm perfectly happy without it."

"But that's part of a relationship." He pressed the palm of his hands against his eyes.

"Most of them, yeah, but not all of them." I bit down on my lower lip, not sure I was getting my point across. "Look, Josh. I've never wanted sex. Ever. Just like I haven't ever wanted to be this close to another person. You're the first person I've been interested in, in my entire life. I'm not ruling sex out completely. I might be willing to try it out, sometime in the future, but for now... it honestly holds no appeal to me. I don't want to do it. You don't want to force me, do you?" That might be harsh, considering his past, but I needed to get it through to him.

"No, of course not." He finally dropped his arms to his lap. His face was all red and blotchy and wet with tears, but his eyes seemed greener than ever with new tears welling up in them. "I would never do that. To anyone."

I wiped more tears away with my thumbs and stared directly into his eyes. "Stop comparing us to everyone else. We're not them, and they're not us. They've got their way of being, and we've got ours. We don't need to be, like, all over each other, or have to jump into bed at every opportunity. There's so much more to life than that.

"I enjoy being with you and sharing a bed with you. Waking up with you in the morning. All of that is because I like you, Josh. Because I like you a lot. I like you more than a lot. And you're the only one, because I couldn't ever do this with anyone else. It feels natural with you, like we've got this connection. I know we do. And I guess that's our thing. We can be together despite not being all over each other. Despite not having sex. Because that's not what it's about. Not for me, anyway, and not for you either."

His eyes flickered between mine, but the tears had subsided a bit.

"Sex has been a bad thing for you for so many years. Doesn't matter if you liked it or not, because the body does respond to things that are good. But the actions itself... they're bad. I think we're perfect because you need something that isn't sex in your life… and I don't want sex in mine at all. So I can give that something to you."

He was silent, but he kept on staring at me, breathing heavily.

"You understand what I'm saying?" I desperately wanted him to understand. I didn't want to keep going in circles, having the same conversations over and over. Sex just wasn't on the table—and he needed to understand why, both for his own sake and for mine.

He nodded jerkily. I wasn't sure I believed it though.

"What about kissing?"

"What about it?"

His lower lip trembled, as if he were close to tears again. "That's part of an intimate relationship. Don't you like that either?"

"Kissing's… fine." I didn't have any other words for it.

"But I'm always the one who kisses you. You never kiss me. And when I do kiss you, it's always chaste. Not any kind of passion to it."

I was back to chewing my lower lip. "You're the only person I've ever kissed too. You're my first everything. I'm new to it. I don't know how things like this work."

He sniffled. "They work both ways. If you want

to kiss me, you can kiss me. I want to kiss you all the time, but I never know if you want to or not, so I just..." He shrugged helplessly. "Often I just leave it be."

"I didn't know kissing was so important to you." I'd thought just being together, being around each other, had been enough. Clearly I'd been wrong.

"Kissing's the one thing that I haven't done tons of. Andrew—it wasn't about love and intimacy with him. He either wanted to fuck me or he wanted to hurt me. Often both at the same time. And all the other blokes I've been with... they've been all about shagging me. My mouth's no good unless it's wrapped around their cocks."

I flinched a bit at his crude words—and the images they procured. I didn't like the thought of Josh being used and abused by his stepfather any more than I did the thought of him being with someone else.

I'd done extensive research on borderline.

Sentences came back to me now as I crouched in front of him, looking up into his cried out, lovely face.

A borderline has a great need for genuine affection. They need to feel loved. They need regular reinforcement in the form of tenderly expressed physical affection and a genuine interest in and respect of their persona.

And another sentence that scared me.

Borderliners do very badly with people who are unable to regularly express affection.

I didn't know how to express affection. I'd never done it before. I was on shaky ground, and I was failing and learning from it.

I went over to the counter to get a few napkins from the dispenser. "Here, clean yourself up a bit." I held them out to Josh.

He took them gingerly, wiped over his face and dabbed at his eyes, then blew his nose. He got up himself to throw it in the rubbish, even though I'd been standing ready to do it for him.

I turned and blocked his direct path back to the chair. "Josh." I stared at him, at how his eyes were sore and his face was all puffed and red. He might be cried out, but that didn't make him any less beautiful to me.

I put my hands on his shoulders and slowly drew him in close to me. He stepped in willingly, leaning against me. I wrapped my arms around him, holding him tight.

"I know some would say it's real fast, but I'm falling in love with you," he mumbled against my shoulder. "I really am."

"Me too," I muttered. "You, I mean." I wasn't good with words, and all the words I'd told him earlier had left me drained. Besides, I'd never been able to say the word *love* out loud, not even to the family I had left.

"This is going to continue, you know," he said, voice still a mumble. "I'm going to doubt you and us. I am aware of just how abnormal I am, but I can't do anything about it."

"It won't have to continue if I can do better at showing you how I feel." I tangled my hand in the hair on his neck, twining the blond strands in-between my fingers. "This is new to me. I'm going to mess it up, I know I am. But I do like you and I am going to do my best to show it to you every day. I promise you that, Josh."

His arms, which had been hanging loosely at his side, now came up to grip the back of my shirt tightly. He clung to me, not saying a single word, but he didn't have to. I understood.

He was messed up. He even had a disorder to prove it.

I had no such thing, but I was messed up too. I should tell him about it—but I couldn't get the words out. It was too hard. I could hardly talk to my therapist about it, and she already knew it all.

I pushed him out from me eventually. Not so much we had to separate, but just enough that I could look into his eyes, could see his lips parted slightly.

He liked kissing, and I'd discovered that so did I. I couldn't give him sex, I didn't want to give him sex. But I could give him this.

I leaned in, uncertain and awkward, because I had never initiated a kiss between us before. I heard him draw in a breath—and then our lips fused together.

He clung tighter to me and I cupped my hands around his neck, thumbs brushing his jaw.

I might've initiated the kiss, but he was in charge of it. Lips on lips I was cool with, but when he tried to take it further, I was on shaky ground again. I parted my lips though, welcomed his tongue, and just let him lead, let him show me what to do next.

And the best thing of all was it was good. So good to kiss him like this, to be so close and so intimate with him.

This time last month I never would've expected to be in this position.

Now that I was, I couldn't imagine going back to how it had been before.

Once we drew back, it took a few seconds for Josh's eyes to flutter back open. They were still shiny from tears, but they'd stopped falling, and a small, shy smile spread over his lips.

"No one's ever kissed me like that before," he whispered.

I leaned in for another quick, chaste kiss, simply because I couldn't help myself.

"Want to wait here while I go change and turn everything off?"

Josh nodded and sat back down on the chair.

I stuffed my apron and shirt in my locker, put on my jumper and jacket, then turned off all lights on my way back out to him.

He rose when I turned off the last light switch and we walked outside together. I locked up, pocketed the keys, and turned to him.

The incident from earlier replayed in my mind. "Hey, does your mum know my boss?"

"What? No. I don't think so." Josh looked at me. "Why?"

"Oh, nothing." I shook my head. It was perfectly logical that they knew each other without Josh knowing it. I had no idea who my uncle and aunt's friends were, after all.

Josh smiled at me as he shyly reached for my hand.

I wasn't sure how to feel about holding hands with someone out in public, but it was late and dark and no one was around.

So I tangled my fingers with his as we started walking home.

CHAPTER 21

JOSH

I walked right over to the sinks so I could stare at myself in the mirror.

I was pale and my eyes looked wide.

Being back at college was terrifying. More so that it was a new school I'd started in, since I'd decided not to go back to the one I'd failed in. I hadn't had any friends there, but it would've felt weird being in the same year as the people who'd taken their first when I'd failed my second.

Still, being in a new college didn't feel any better. I didn't know anyone here either, but it didn't make me any more confident about the first day.

A sob echoed through the toilets and I froze.

I turned my head slowly, eyes darting over the

open stalls. The door of the last one was closed, and another sob could be heard from behind it.

I wasn't sure if I should leave or not.

Before I could make a decision, I heard the door being unlocked, and then a small body dressed in clothes that were at least two sizes too big, stepped out. He sniffled, tears drying on his cheeks, and he was *familiar*.

"*Mal?*"

He whirled around, cowering back against the wall. His arm came up, like he was either ready to defend himself or to try and block a hit to his face.

"Mal, it's me. Josh." I took a step closer to him.

Wild eyes met mine and recognition sparked. His arm dropped and he straightened up a bit more as he eyed me warily.

"Hey." I hadn't seen him since I'd last talked to him in group. He'd been hospitalised for the last couple of weeks. "I didn't know you went to college here."

I wouldn't say Mal was relaxed, but he wasn't as tightly coiled as he'd been before he'd recognised me either. "I didn't know you did."

"I have to retake the last year, you know, and I decide to switch colleges. I didn't want to continue at the old one." I'd talked about failing my last year in group, so he knew all about it.

He only nodded.

"Do you want to have lunch with me?" Just as he knew all about me, I also knew all about him. I remembered clearly all the times he'd relayed being bullied in group—and that bullying had taken place at school.

"Can we go outside?" He was wary.

"Sure." I shrugged like it wasn't a big deal. It wasn't either, I didn't mind going outside. But I knew the reason he wanted to, and it wasn't because the weather was nice.

It wasn't until school was over I witnessed just what Mal had to go through. A gang of lads had cornered him just outside the college. At first, I only heard them yelling. Then I saw Mal cowering against the wall, much in the same way he'd done in the toilets with me.

Mal tried to leave, to walk past them with his head down, but they shoved him back so hard the back of his head connected with the wall.

Mal crumbled to the ground, arms going up to protect his head.

The gang of lads laughed at him and shoved playfully at each other.

Then they simply walked away.

The last of them gave Mal a proper kick to the gut.

"Mal!" I ran over to him.

"G-go a-away!" He pushed to his feet, inched around me like he was afraid to touch me, and then he ran away.

I turned to look after him, but I didn't make a move to follow or call after him. I knew what it was like needing to get away.

I'd try talking to him again tomorrow. Either in school or in group.

CHAPTER 22

"*K*ian?"

He stood in front of our door, just staring at it.

He jerked around in surprise. "Oh, Damian, hey." He shuffled his feet.

I hoisted my shoulder bag further up on my shoulder. It was crammed full of books.

"Nobody home?" I cast a curious glance at the door.

"I don't know." Kian glanced at it too. "I haven't knocked yet." He seemed out of sorts.

I brushed past him, giving him an odd look as I did so. It swung open with no resistance, not locked at all. I went inside, but Kian still stood outside.

"You coming in?" I eyed him curiously now.

He hesitated, but he slowly walked inside, allowing me to close the door. He looked around, and my guess would likely be correct in that he was looking for Silver.

I headed into my bedroom, leaving him there to deal with whatever it was.

Josh was sitting curled up on my bed, head bowed and looking dejected.

I stopped just inside the threshold.

"Hi. You all right?" I finally let my shoulder bag slide off my shoulder and thud to the floor.

Josh's eyes were sad when he looked up at me and my chest squeezed. "I'm fine. I'm just—It's Mal."

"Mal?" I frowned. Who was Mal?

I went over to sit on the bed too.

"He's in my group. Today it turned out that we also go to the same college." Josh's hands twisted in his lap. "He's bullied. I saw it myself when the day was over. At lunch he was crying in the toilets. They're real mean to him—and I know what he goes through and it's not fair that college should be shit for him too."

I didn't know what to say, as per usual. I didn't know this person and I didn't know what he wanted me to say to it. Maybe he didn't want me to say anything at all. Maybe he just needed to talk about it.

"Mal's like me. Borderline, like I am." He shook

his head. "I shouldn't talk about this. I'm not really allowed to. Group rules and all that. But we're in the same college now, in the same year. It's just not fair."

"You could be his friend," I suggested, in lack of anything else. "Sounds like he needs one of those."

"Yeah. If he'll let me." Josh's hand fluttered out to his side to settle atop his journal.

I smiled to myself as I saw it. He wrote in it frequently and he kept it around like it was a treasure. For me it had only been a book too pretty to use for anything.

"He'll be lucky to have you as a friend."

Josh's eyes lit up at that. "You think so?"

"I do." I leaned in to kiss him. I'd got rather good at showing him affection, at least in private. We hadn't had another bout of crying or a conversation about it, after all, so I was pretty sure I was doing okay. "How was your first day, aside from that bloke?"

He shrugged. "It was okay. I've been through it before. I did well at the beginning of last year before everything went to shit again. I reckon I'm properly ahead of most of them." He leaned in for another kiss. "How was your day?"

"Uneventful. It was all mostly information and such. I bought all my books though. Nearly broke my back bringing them home." I motioned to my discarded shoulder bag.

"That's a lot of books."

"That's what I have to look forward to for years now." I lay down on the bed, on my stomach, resting my chin on the back of my hands.

"You've never told me what kind of surgeon you want to be." Josh lay down next to me.

"I've been thinking about Plastics. Like, reconstructive surgery and all that." I wanted to help people like him, people with scars. People like *me*.

"I wish I knew what I wanted to do." Josh blew out a wistful breath.

"You'll figure it out."

He leaned in to rest his head against my shoulder. "If you want me to stay the night at home sometimes, you have to tell me."

"What?" Where'd that come from?

"I mean, it's like I'm living here. I'm sleeping here every night, coming straight here after college or group or therapy or whatever I'm doing. I've not spent a night in my own bed in… I can't even remember the last time I spent the night at home."

"I don't mind you being here. Not at all. I like it." Surprisingly enough. But I'd had him around for almost a month now. It would be a month in two days.

"Can I call you my boyfriend?" The question came out all hesitant.

I frowned down at the sheets. "I guess."

"We are in a relationship, aren't we? I'm not doing anything with anyone else. It's only you. Don't you feel the same way?"

"I do." Of course I did. "Yeah. Yeah, I guess we're boyfriends. I've just never thought about labelling it."

"You don't like to label yourself?"

I shrugged. It was a bit awkward, considering he still had his head resting on my shoulder. "I don't know. I guess. Silver keeps referring to me being asexual. I've always gone with it, because I guess it's true. He also mentioned you being my boyfriend once, but that was when we'd just met, so I guess we weren't back then."

"But we are now?" he prodded.

"Yeah. We are."

"I've been wanting to ask you for a while."

"Why haven't you?"

"I was afraid of the answer." That came out in a whisper.

I turned my head to the side. It was awkward, but I could see his face. "Why? We've been close ever since the day we met. I'm closer to you than I've ever been to anyone. I've told you this."

"I know you have. I'm sorry. I doubt things. It's what I do." He went from hesitant to dejected in a second.

"Josh." I sighed. I reached back, gently removed his head off my shoulder and pushed him down on the bed so I could finally look at him properly. "You need to stop doubting everything." I stroked my hand over his cheek.

He stared up at me. Then he grabbed me around the neck and applied pressure, and I fell willingly down into the kiss.

It was absurd how much I liked kissing him, considering I'd never liked close contact with anyone. Everything was so different with Josh. And I wasn't complaining at all.

SILVER SAT at the table when I ventured into the kitchen for something to drink.

"Hey, mate, what's the etiquette for monthly anniversaries?" I asked. The thought had been on my mind since I'd realised it was only two days until we'd known each other a month. "Is something expected of a monthly anniversary or—" I'd turned to face him and shut myself up when I saw the look on his face. "Is everything all right?"

Silver dragged his hands over his face. "Kian came with some bad news today. Still trying to process it properly."

Uh oh. "He broke up with you?"

Silver shook his head. "He might've been exposed to HIV."

I sank down opposite him. "HIV?"

"Yeah. This bloke he pulled once a while ago looked him up today. He's got HIV and he's not sure if he got it before or after Kian sucked him off."

Ah, Jesus. Did everyone have to be so blunt about the sex talk? "And?"

"And he might be infected. If he is, I am."

"You haven't been safe?" I might not be interested in sex at all, but I darn well knew what a condom was for.

Silver shook his head again. "Not on oral."

I stared at him, unimpressed. "What's the point of being safe with one thing and not the other?"

He looked properly chastised. "What can I say, D. It's passion. When you're going to fuck someone, condoms are part of the equation. But when you're pulling their pants down and got a dick slap you in the face, you just want to go down on it, you know. Condoms aren't exactly forefront of the mind in that moment. Latex tastes like shit anyway."

"Silver." I had a sudden need to cover my ears

with my hands, but I managed to refrain from it. I wasn't a fourteen-year-old girl, after all.

"Right. Sorry." He held his palms up towards me. "Anyway, we're going to go get tested in the morning. I guess we'll find out then."

"You seem pretty chilled about it. I mean, it's a disease you will have to live with your entire life. One that will change your entire life."

Silver leaned back in his chair, his eyes staring up at the ceiling for a moment before settling back on me. "I am freaking out. A little bit. Of course I am. But at the same time, we should've been more careful, so ultimately it's our fault. It's the risk of sex, anyway. Everyone who has it risks exposing themselves to HIV." He eyed me up and down. "You're lucky. You never have to worry about it. Or has that changed?"

"It hasn't," I deadpanned.

"How does your boyfriend feel about that?" He grinned now. Josh's moods weren't the only ones that changed quickly.

I refused to answer that. "If you're not going to be serious, I'm going to walk away."

He chuckled and crossed his arms over his chest. "It's just a month. Do something simple, something sweet. Flowers or some shit."

"What? Flowers?" I could feel the grimace.

Silver was full-out laughing now. "Now, when it's the one-year anniversary, that's when you have to pull out the big guns."

One year? He sure was jumping ahead.

"Where is Josh?"

"In bed." He was writing in his journal. "Where's Kian?"

Silver's grin dimmed. "He went home. Said it would be best for us to spend the night apart. You know, temptation and all that."

I didn't know actually, but I refrained from saying that.

He knew, anyway.

I got back up to fix myself a glass of water. "Good luck tomorrow, I guess?"

He groaned. "Yeah. I guess we need that."

I eyed him out of the corner of my eye. "I'm sure it'll be fine. If that bloke doesn't even know when he contracted it, it's a big possibility it happened after Kian, and then everything should be fine."

"Sure hope you're right."

"You should be more careful."

He turned sheepish. "Yeah."

"I never thought I'd have to tell you that."

"I've never been so madly in lust with someone before."

My eyebrows rose.

"Well, you know." He shrugged. "We're very physical. I really like him. This could be *it*, you know."

"Have you told Kian?"

"Told him? About what?" It dawned on him the moment the questions were out, and he got a dark look in his eyes. "No."

"He hasn't seen your back?" I found that hard to believe.

"He asked about it."

Silver's whole back was a memorial tattoo.

He narrowed his eyes at me. "Have *you* told Josh?"

"No. Fair enough." I took my water with me and made for the door. "I really hope tomorrow goes well for you. For you both."

"Thanks, mate. Appreciated."

Josh looked up from his journal when I came back in my room.

"That was a long trip to get some water."

I put my glass on the bedside table, then fell down on the bed. "I had a chat with Silver."

Josh closed his journal and turned around so he could rest against me. "I like lying like this with you."

"Me too." I carded my fingers through his hair. "This is nice."

SEPTEMBER 3RD

I asked.

And he said yes.

Boyfriends. The word has a strange sound to it. I've never had a boyfriend before. And now I do.

I've got a boyfriend.

I'VE GOT A BOYFRIEND.

SEPTEMBER 4TH

So apparently Silver and Kian had a HIV scare?

That turned out to be negative. Thankfully.

I can't help but think I've been lucky. I could've had it. Ten years of abuse could've left me with a lot, a lot that isn't mental illness, and HIV is one of those things. And I wasn't exactly careful when I hooked up with other people either.

So I've been lucky.

What would I have done if I'd been positive?

I sure wouldn't have been in the situation I'm in now.

Who wants someone with both mental illness and HIV, after all?

Though, if you're not having sex, I guess the HIV status doesn't really matter that much?

Not that this entire entry matters because I'm negative. And Silver and Kian are both negative. We're all negative.

Thank God for that.

SEPTEMBER 12TH

Mal keeps dodging me before and after school, but he's perfectly happy to sit with me outside for lunch. I don't know why he does it. Maybe the bullies are worse at those particular times?

They usually stay away from him at lunch. I don't know why. I would think lunch hour would be a perfect time to torture him like they do, but maybe they're too busy actually eating.

I tried to get Mal to tell on them.

He wouldn't do it.

He says he's dealing.

He even said so in group—and we're not supposed to lie in group. But I know people do. I know I do. There're just certain things you don't want anyone to know.

So we usually spend lunch together. It's nice, though we don't really talk much.

I don't know what I've done to be so lucky. Maybe after ten years of hell, and then dealing with that hell with more hell, has left karma on my side?

I've not only got a boyfriend, but I think I've got friends as well.

Silver, obviously, but he's kind of a packaged deal with Damian, being his best friend and all. But Kian is lovely—and I think he likes me. And then there's Spencer and Leslie. They're great lads, kind and including.

Mal too. I like to think of him as my friend. I know it's against group rules. It's supposed to be unhealthy for group members if there's intimacy between some of them. But it's not like Mal and I are intimate. We just sit together at lunch, because we go to the same college.

We only share about our lives in group. We know each other so well because of it, but it's not something we ever talk about at lunch. We don't have deep conversation about all the shit in our lives.

We just sit together. Sometimes in silence, sometimes we talk about school stuff or something equally neutral.

It's nice to have friends. To have a boyfriend who's kind and who seems to both like and respect me. At least that's what he says.

I can't keep myself from wondering just how long it'll last though.

It certainly can't last forever. I know it won't.

Karma will turn at one point and bitch slap me in the face again. Like she usually does.

OCTOBER 8TH

I'm starting to have to study a lot more now.

Last year was good at first, then everything went to shit with depression and self-harm and hospitalisations. I don't want to be that wreck this year. I want to finish, with grades I can be proud of. At least grades that will keep me from having to retake another year.

I don't think I can take that.

Damian's got a lot more to do though. He usually stays late at school to study in the library. When he's home, he's usually got his head buried in a book.

The rational part of me understands that it's med-school, that it's his future career, and he's doing his best to be good at it. To be excellent at it.

The other part, the biggest and the messed up part of me, switches between being sad and being jealous. I want him to spend more time with me. We'd spent so much time together the month before school started and it had been wonderful.

And now we only see each other early in the mornings and late evenings.

It's hard.

Saying anything else would be lying. And I'm not supposed to lie. I'm supposed to be honest about my feelings, but I can't be to him, because then he'll be guilty. I want him to do well in school.

I just wish there was time for quality time with me as well.

CHAPTER 23

DAMIAN

*I*t snuck up on me.

I was busy with course work, and trying to spend the rest of my time either working or with Josh.

Then one day my eyes fell on the calendar.

Seeing the red circle felt like being hit in the chest with a sledgehammer.

For over half the month I'd been so busy I hadn't even noticed someone had turned the calendar over to October. And now the red circle I always put on that particular date once I bought a new calendar glared at me.

I stumbled back and caught myself on the counter. I gripped it tight and then slid to the floor when my knees couldn't keep me up anymore.

My eyes were glued to the date.

That fucking date.

Why did I keep circling it every bloody year?

Because if I didn't it would sneak up and hit me like a bulldozer on the particular day, and that always made it so much worse.

When September was over and I turned the calendar over, at least I knew I'd have over twenty days to prepare.

But I'd been so busy I hadn't even had chance to look at the calendar once.

But now half the term was about to be over and I wasn't as busy as I'd been, and there it was... the red circle, standing out against the white and the black.

Mocking me, was what it felt like.

I hated that day. It was the day my whole life had changed. It might've been for the better, but the way it'd happened... that wasn't good at all. It was horrible and something I wish I could just forget, because thinking about it always left me a mess.

There was a reason I always kept those memories locked away good and proper in the back of my mind.

"Damian?"

I could see Josh enter the kitchen out of the corner of my eye.

No, no, no.

He was home already?

"Are you okay?" He came over to me, voice concerned.

No, no, no.

He couldn't be here.

Not now.

My mind was overflowing by those horrid memories.

"Damian? You're scaring me." He put his hand on my arm.

Something normally so innocent made my body move in a flurry now. Without really knowing it was going to happen, I'd pushed him away from me, so hard he fell back on the floor.

"Don't touch me!" I pushed to my feet next.

I knew I'd done something wrong, something possibly irreversible. I could see it in the stricken look on his face.

But there was one time in the year I couldn't be strong and it was *now*.

Death, death, death.

I didn't want to remember.

I didn't want to see it flash through my mind again, like it did every year.

"I can't—I need to be alone right now." I didn't

look at him again as I hurried out of the room to lock myself in my bedroom.

I didn't even turn the lights on. I just sunk to the floor and buried my face against my kneecaps.

CHAPTER 24

JOSH

For a beat I didn't move.

I couldn't move. It was like I was frozen to the floor.

What had I done wrong? What had I done to cause that reaction from him? I'd been good lately. I hadn't even cut myself.

He, who was kind and gentle and patient with me… he'd pushed me. Pushed me away hard.

I went from frozen to a flurry of movement. I walked out to the living room, where I shrugged on my rucksack, and then I left.

I couldn't stay there. He'd specifically told me he wanted to be alone.

So I would leave him alone.

He'd *pushed* me away. He'd never done anything

to hurt me before, and now he'd suddenly got physical. It didn't make sense. I didn't know why.

I felt numb all over.

I couldn't even cry—and I was a master at that.

Mum wasn't home when I got there. It was too early for her to be off work yet. So I dropped my rucksack and shoes in the hallway and headed for my room.

I didn't know how long I sat on my bed.

All I knew was I felt the numbness spread. Eventually it was like I couldn't even move my fingers. Everything was numb, to body functions, to my feelings, to my bloody damaged brain.

And I hated it. I hated the numbness.

I couldn't remember finding the razor. All I knew was I'd been sitting on the bed, then my jumper was off and the cold metal slashed into my skin.

I was relentless.

I wanted to feel *something*.

Even if it was pain, it was better than nothing.

"Joshua?" There was a knock on my door. "I saw your rucksack. Are you in there? I need to talk to you. Tell you something."

A sob escaped me and I curled in on myself. There were no tears, but that didn't seem to stop the sob.

She must've heard it, because she opened the door.

I tilted my head to look up at her and I could see how she visibly flinched once she got a look at me.

"Joshua." She drew in a shaking breath.

I turned my head back to the floor. It was dotted with pools of blood. Blood had been flying everywhere.

"Oh my God." She came closer. "Joshua." She crouched down next to me, hand landing tentatively on my back.

"I think I need to go to A&E." My voice was flat. Yet still shaking a tiny bit. "I think I might need sutures."

She rose again and left the room, and for a minute there I felt completely abandoned. So much so that feelings returned—along with the tears. But she came back quickly and she had two towels she wrapped around both of my arms.

"Keep them there. Try to press on it. I'm driving you right now."

She helped me stand. I kept my arms crossed and pressed to my chest as she guided me outside to her car. She even tied my shoes in the hallway, because I couldn't do it myself.

The car ride was silent. My forehead was pressed

against the cool window and I watched buildings fly past as she drove a bit faster than the speed limit.

I was silent when we entered the A&E, and also when I was taken back and my arms were cleaned up and sutured.

I didn't say a word until we were on our way back home again.

"I think I want to go to Bristol." I sniffled.

"You think?" She was steadfastly watching the road.

"I *want* to. I want to go. Get away."

"It's your decision, Joshua. If you want to go, I can buy you a train ticket. Or I could drive you down. It's the weekend. I don't have to go back to work until Monday. And for you it's half-term so you've got the next week off."

"Maybe we could drive?" Just me and her, on a road trip. It sounded a lot more appealing than sitting on a train surrounded by strangers.

I saw out of the corner of my eye that she nodded. "You want to leave right now?"

"Yeah." I didn't want to stay.

What did I have to stay at home for?

She nodded again. "Then we'll go home and pack each of our bags."

Gratefulness bloomed in my chest.

I squeezed my eyes shut to stop the tears. I hadn't

been crying much lately, because I'd thought I'd been happy, but now… what was happiness? I wasn't sure I could ever be properly happy.

"Thanks, Mum."

She reached over to squeeze my hand. "Anything for you, Joshua. Anything."

CHAPTER 25

DAMIAN

I'd managed to fall asleep, though it hadn't exactly been a peaceful one. I hadn't been plagued by the kind of nightmares Josh usually had, but they'd been there. Everything had happened in my dream, exactly like it had as I could remember, and it had felt so real. It hadn't felt like a nightmare at all.

I hadn't woken up screaming or shaking or terrified like Josh used to.

The dream had simply continued on, until I'd suddenly opened my eyes.

I lay for a while, trying to figure out what had woken me. I could hear people moving around in the living room and bathroom, so I reckoned Silver was home from work.

I could hear muffled voices. I hoped he was talking to Josh, that he was keeping Josh's mood up.

Shit. I pushed him.

I got out of bed and padded over to the door. I was disappointed when it opened though because it wasn't Josh on the sofa, but Kian.

Silver came out the bathroom the moment I opened the door and his smile died a slow death once he got a good look at me.

"Hey, mate. All right?"

I looked into the kitchen. Empty. "Where's Josh?"

"Not here. I thought he was in there with you." He motioned to my room.

I shook my head slowly, then pressed my palms to my face.

Shit, shit, shit.

"Mate, what's wrong?"

"I pushed him away." The words were hard to get out. I was ashamed of what I'd done to him.

Silver frowned. "What'd you mean?"

"I physically pushed him." I let my arms drop and cast him a desperate look. "It's in four days, and I just realised it. He came upon me and I *pushed* him."

It was dawning on Silver. "You forgot the date?"

"Yeah." I got cold all of a sudden, and I wrapped my arms around myself. "I was freaking out. I still am, a little bit. And he had to come in at that exact moment, and he was just being worried, like, and I pushed him away."

Kian looked at me from over the back of the sofa. "Just ring him, mate. Explain that it was a shitty time, and apologise. I'm sure it'll be fine."

I started to shake my head before he'd even finished speaking. "You don't understand." I pressed the back of my hands to my eyes. "What I just did… it's bad. So bad."

"Josh's a sweet bloke. Surely he'll understand you didn't mean anything by it." Kian frowned now too.

He didn't understand. He didn't know about Josh's issues, about him being borderline and what that entailed.

I cast a wild glance at Silver, who looked back at me with an emotion I couldn't decipher. I was so bad at that. It could be pity, or sadness, or understanding. Besides me, Silver was the one closest to Josh—and Silver knew everything that had happened since I'd met him.

"You should go speak to him in person. He probably went home to his mum's. He hasn't got anywhere else to go, has he?"

"No." Josh only had his mum—and me. And I'd failed him.

"The quicker you go talk to him, the quicker this'll be solved. Nothing like this has happened before, so if you apologise—and explain—I'm sure Josh will understand. If anyone should understand your feelings about your past, it's him. You need to *tell* him. You should've told him long before October came around."

"I've been so busy, I wasn't aware of the dates. That they were getting so close to-to—" I couldn't even say it. After all these years and I was still incapable of *saying* it.

"I remember around this time last year. We'd met only a month and a half before. I knew something was up with you but I had no idea what. And I didn't feel like I knew you enough to ask. But when you finally told me, I understood what it was all about. So will Josh."

"No, Silver. You don't get it. I did something bad, and that will affect him. You know borderliners have a black-and-white thinking pattern. I might've been white—but now I'm going to be all black."

"You've been together for two and a half months. Surely that can't apply to you anymore?"

"It applies to *everyone*. A single little word can do it. And I physically *pushed* him away from me. He fell because of me. And I told him I needed to be alone. That's more than enough reason for his thoughts to switch around to the other opposite."

"Go talk to him *now*." Silver slapped my shoulder.

"If it is that bad, you can't waste a bloody second, D. Go to him, tell him everything, no matter how fucking hard it is. You managed to tell me. Surely you can tell him."

I wasn't so sure about that, but I went.

But when I got there, no one was home.

And when I finally tried to ring him—no one answered.

CHAPTER 26

JOSH

*M*um and I stayed with Grandma the night we arrived. She was surprised, but happily so, when we showed up on her doorstep.

I went to visit Cooper the next day, simply because he was the only one of my cousins I knew enough to actually have a proper conversation with.

He opened the door, looking like shit and yawning wide.

"Josh?" He peered at me. "What're you doing here?"

"Mum and I came down for a visit." He was bare-chested, and his joggers hung so far down his hips I was afraid to dip my eyes down lower in case everything was on display.

"Come in, come in." He waved me inside.

Cooper had a small flat: just a tiny living room with a kitchen, bathroom, toilet, and an equally tiny bedroom. It was enough for him though.

"Can I get you anything? I might have some Sprite, if I didn't finish it off last night." He looked in the fridge.

"I don't need anything, thanks." I wasn't thirsty. All I wanted was something else to think about.

"I literally can't remember how I got home last night." Copper dropped down next to me. "I think maybe Kale dropped my drunk arse back here. He's all responsible like that."

"New boyfriend?" The name didn't ring a bell with me.

He threw me an unimpressed glare. "My best mate. My *straight* best mate."

"Oh." I'd heard about him a few times. I wasn't sure Cooper had ever mentioned him by name though.

"So what's up?" Cooper's knee bumped mine. "I thought you were all shacked up with your new boyfriend. Where's he?"

"Back in London." I didn't want to talk about it. I wanted to forget. "I'm not sure he's my boyfriend anymore."

"Why not?" He bumped my knee again.

"Cooper." I wasn't here to unload on him.

"Look, you tell me your woes, I'll tell you mine."

I cast him a wry look. "You've got woes?" I did the universal sign for quotes on the last word. It wasn't a word I'd ever used before. Maybe if I'd lived in Shakespeare's time.

"They might even trump yours."

Cooper was a person who was outgoing and always the life of the party. Always had a smile. But now he was serious and I found myself believing him. Because Cooper was never serious about anything. That was the main thing that could make him get on everyone's nerves.

"It's not much to tell, really," I said. "He pushed me, told me he needed to be alone, and I ended up at A&E, having to get sutures on both of my arms."

"He *pushed* you?" Cooper sounded scandalised. "Why the hell did he do that?"

"Don't know." He hadn't exactly given me a reason for it, had he?

"I hope you're not going to take it? That's the beginning of abuse that is."

"What—No!" My head whipped around to face him. "He's not like that. Something had happened and he couldn't stand for me to touch him. I don't know what'd happened, but something did."

Cooper wasn't convinced. "If I had a boyfriend,

who pushed me, I would've run the other way. I'm no one's punching bag."

"Neither am I." I was getting upset. I didn't like the way he was taking what I'd said. "He would never hurt me, Coop. It was an accident."

"That's what they *all* say." He crossed his arms defensively.

My eyes narrowed. "Have you been pushed around?"

He shrugged.

I took that as a yes.

"Look. Damian is the sweetest bloke. But he hasn't told me his story and there's something there. I know it's difficult. Otherwise why would he keep it back, right? So, I think it's bad. Maybe not my kind of bad, but I definitely think it's bad."

Cooper sighed. He loosened a bit, which I was grateful for. "I don't know him. You know best. I guess I'm the loser who falls for all the arseholes."

I didn't know what to say to that. "Why don't you live at home? Wouldn't you save money?" That was a question I'd been wondering about since I'd heard he'd moved out. I hadn't had time to ask, or even think about it while they'd been in London though.

"If I lived at home, I wouldn't be able to live my life the way I want to live it. Mum's got all the rules and stuff, and I just can't get with that. I'm old enough to decide for myself, not have her running around telling me what I can and can't do." He cleared his throat, then imitated Aunt Abigail's voice to his best ability. *"You can't keep partying like you are, Cooper, it's not good for you. You can't keep sleeping around like you do, Cooper, you'll end up catching something you can't be rid of. You can't do this, Cooper, you can't do that, Cooper."* He groaned in annoyance. "You see, I can't live with that. It's my life and I got to live it whilst I still can. It's not like I have long left, after all."

My head whipped around to face him again.

Fear stuck in me, like a dagger being turned in my chest. "Cooper, you aren't—are you?" I couldn't say the word. Strange, as I'd attempted it myself and I had no problem using it in sessions with Vincent or in group.

He blinked at me. "You mean suicidal?" It dawned on him rather quickly. He laughed. "No, mate. Hardly that. But I do have numbered days."

"Are you sick?" Mum hadn't said anything about Cooper being ill. If there'd been something life-threatening, surely the family would know?

"See, Josh, that's my woe. My life will change. I don't know when, all I know is it will. It can happen in a minute, in days, in years. There's just no way of knowing. All I know is my sight's getting worse and there's nothing I can do about."

His sight? "What'd you mean?"

"I've got this eye disease. My sight is steadily growing worse and eventually it'll be so bad I won't be able to see shit." He stared at me, all serious. "I'll be blind eventually."

I swallowed heavily. "Who knows about it?"

"No one," he deadpanned. "Well, Kale knows. And now you. But besides the two of you, no one. And I would like it to stay that way."

"You don't want the rest of the family to know?" I was startled. I hadn't wanted anyone to know about what Andrew had been doing to me, but my circumstances had been vastly different from his. He had a disease that would blind him. Why didn't he want his family's support?

"Nope." He shook his head for emphasis. "It's none of their business. They're judging me and my lifestyle, and they can just keep doing it. I don't care. I'm the black sheep of the family, after all. Why make them get rid of that label when it fits so well?"

Cooper might act all tough, but I would bet he was secretly ashamed on the inside.

That's what I had been.

I'd wanted to die before I let anyone know. I'd failed at it, and they'd all found out, but they'd all been there for me. They all took time off work to come down to London to support me through the last part of the trial.

I appreciated that, even if I hadn't been able to be around them much.

Maybe that was why Cooper didn't want them to know, too—because they could be *too* much. His sister especially. She could be rude at times, and outspoken, and not even realise she was hurting other peoples' feelings.

"So that's my secret. Now that that's out of the way... what are your plans for the day?" Cooper seemed to just throw the entire issue over his shoulder and forget about it. I didn't know how he did it, but I wish I had that ability.

"I'm going out to eat with Mum later. She's got something she wants to tell me." I had no idea what it was. She hadn't given me a single hint. I hoped it wasn't something bad. I couldn't take more bad things happening.

"Want to come out with me tonight? Check out the nightlife here in Bristol?" He grinned.

My eyebrows rose. "Weren't you out last night?"

"Yeah."

"And you want to go out tonight? Two days in a row?"

"I always go out two days in a row. Fridays and

Saturdays. It's standard." Now he was looking at me as if I was the mad one.

I knew he liked to party... but two days in a row, *every* week? That seemed like quite a lot. Considering I hardly ever went out anymore, it sounded absurd.

"Yeah. I'll come out with you." I'd never been out in Bristol, after all, and what else did I have to do?

"Newly single and everything." He clapped my shoulder. "We'll find you a nice shag."

"Wha—No! I'm not... I'm just *not*." We hadn't broken up. *Had we?* I didn't think we had. He'd only said he needed to be alone for a while, not forever. Maybe he'd just needed a break and then we'd be fine again.

Cooper smirked. "Maybe we'll find me a nice shag then."

Now that was more like it.

I COULDN'T HELP but notice Mum was nervous. She kept moving the cutlery around, as if she wasn't happy with the placement of it.

Her apparent nervousness made mine ten-times worse, because if she was nervous about what she had to say... then where would that leave me?

Clearly it was something that would be important

to me, or else she wouldn't be fussing so much about it.

Our food arrived and I started in on it, since it didn't seem like she was about to start talking anytime soon.

"Good?" she asked once she'd taken a bite herself.

"Mhm." I nodded, mouth full of fish. We weren't in the kind of fancy restaurant my mum preferred. We'd settled on a simple fish & chips shop, and I didn't regret it, because it tasted wonderful.

"I think so too." She smiled, but it was shaky at best.

"Whatever you got to say, say it." I put my cutlery down. She was making me too nervous to enjoy it. "I can take it." That could be a possible lie, but until she told me what it was, I hoped I could.

She blew out a breath. She wasn't looking at me, but at a point over my shoulder.

"Spill it. Just say it, Mum. Don't hesitate. Just get it out there." I clenched my hands into fists, afraid of what I was about to hear.

She closed her eyes then finally looked straight at me when she opened them again. "I've met someone."

I reared back so fast the chair almost fell back, but I managed to catch onto the table before both the chair and I tumbled to the floor.

I hadn't known what to expect, but it hadn't been *that*.

"No." I shook my head. "No, no, no." I couldn't stop shaking my head. Last time she'd met someone, *married* someone, my life had turned into an unbearable hell.

"Joshua." She abandoned her seat and came over to crouch down in front of me. She tilted her face up to me, trying to catch my eyes. "This isn't like Andrew. This person… is good. They're not someone who would hurt anyone else."

"I'm sure that's what you thought when you met Andrew too." I pressed my hands against the side of my head as I rocked back and forth on the chair. "He managed to hide it from you for ten years."

She drew in a shaky breath. "You're grown up, Joshua. No matter what, no one can hurt you again. You're not a little defenceless kid anymore."

She was right, of course. It wasn't like I could be forced into something I didn't want to do. Like I had to rely on the one person who kept hurting me in ways I couldn't even explain back then.

I was my own boss now. I wasn't the boy who was scared to death of being home, of being in bed, because I knew it wouldn't be long until I wasn't alone in it.

That wasn't me. I was stronger now.

"Who is it?" I probably wouldn't even know if she told me. I only hoped his name wasn't Andrew Graham—but then that wasn't likely, as he was locked up in prison. He wouldn't get out for a long time.

"Harriet."

"Harriet?" My arms fell down and I stopped the rocking, all because of the shock. "But that's a-a woman's name?"

Mum nodded quickly. "She's a woman, yeah."

"Since when do you like women?"

"I always have. Back in college, and in university before I met Andrew, I mostly had romantic connections with other women. If I went out to pull with my mates, I always ended up with other girls—"

"Oh, yeah, that's enough, thanks." I held my hands up. I wasn't grown up enough to hear about my mum's sexual escapades.

A small smile found its way to her lips. It was actually nice to see, because Mum hadn't smiled much for the last two years.

A memory came back to me, of Damian asking me if my mum knew his boss.

"Harriet. As in *Harriet*? Damian's *boss*?"

"Yeah." She made a single nod. "That's the one. Didn't Damian tell you?"

"He asked if you two knew each other, but that's

all." My eyebrows drew together. "Did he catch you in a compromising position or something?"

"No, not at all. I was just meeting her after work, and we went home together." She was still crouched in front of me, looking up at me. "We're taking things slow. After Andrew... well, I'm a bit cautious after that. But I do like her."

"That's good." I wanted my mum to be happy. That she seemed to be so with another woman didn't faze me at all.

If it'd been a new man in the picture—that might've disturbed me more, but a woman... that was better.

Mum went back to her seat. "She has a nephew who's your age. He's got some issues, and when I told her you were doing well with group therapy, she thought that might be an option for him as well."

I took another piece of fish and chewed it before I answered. "What's his issues?"

"His mum died years ago, but she thinks his lifestyle suggest he's not dealing with it too well. I gave her the contact information for your therapist. Maybe he'll show up in group one day."

"Yeah." There wasn't anything against the rules there, since I didn't know him. He wasn't related to me.

Mum's smile widened. "I was hoping we could

go out to dinner one day, when we're back in London. I want you to meet Harriet properly, and maybe her nephew will come with too. Maybe you can get to know each other?"

"That sounds… nice." It did. But I couldn't help but worry, because going back to London… I didn't want to at the moment. I didn't have anything to go back to.

I'd left, without a word. When Damian had tried to call me last night, I'd only turned the phone on silent and left it at that. I didn't want to know what he had to say. If he was breaking up with me, I'd rather not hear it. I couldn't be responsible for what I'd do if that were to happen.

If he said the words, I knew I couldn't settle on cutting my arms up. If he said them, I knew it would break me. I knew I would have to do something else. Something I'd only attempted once—and utterly failed at.

If he said them, I knew I wouldn't want to fail.

I'd want to do it properly, and I would make sure I did.

So I couldn't hear the words. I couldn't let them break me.

CHAPTER 27

DAMIAN

*I*t was late and I was lying flat on my bed. I stared upwards, but it wasn't the ceiling I saw.

My thoughts were a mess of my past and what had happened with Josh the day before. I'd tried going over to his place again today, but there hadn't been anyone home this time either.

I'd tried to call, but he hadn't picked up.

Shit.

I'd messed it up.

I hoped he was okay, that he hadn't done something or something had happened. I needed him, but I had no idea how to go about getting him back here when he wasn't answering his phone, and no one was at home.

What was I supposed to do?

I had no idea where he was.

I couldn't tell him anything when I couldn't get a hold of him.

Everyone flashed before my eyes. My parents, my sisters, Josh…

I scratched over my chest. My jumper was too thick to feel anything, so I shoved my hand under it and ran it over bare skin. My not-very-smooth skin.

Josh hadn't ever seen my scar. I'd seen his, at least the ones on his arms, but I'd never shown him mine. I'd always been careful not to change in front of him, at least not when I had to get naked to do so.

Something started vibrating next to me and I was halfway off the bed before I realised it was just my mobile.

I stared down at it.

Unknown number flashed on the screen.

I hated answering the phone, especially when I didn't know who rang.

But it could be important.

"Hello?"

"Damian?"

I blinked, trying to place the feminine voice. "Angelina?" My heart started beating at triple speed. *What if something's happened to him?*

"Yes. Hi." She breathed in and out a couple of

time. "I don't know what happened yesterday, but whatever it was he took it hard. I'm not blaming you, Damian. I know better than anyone how just a slight word can have serious consequences with him."

I swallowed heavily. It wasn't just a slight word. It was so much more than that. "I pushed him away from me." It was better to be honest about it. "I— Something bad happened years ago and the date was getting close and I couldn't handle it. And he came in the room and I just—I pushed him."

She was silent for at least half a minute. "I know how that is too. I pushed him away emotionally for the first sixteen years of his life. That played a big part in who he is today. I regret it, but I can't change it. All I can do is try my very best to make it up to him now."

I nodded, even though I knew she couldn't see me. "How is he?"

"He's—" She hesitated. I knew something must've happened. "He's not fine, but he's okay. I think he's scared."

"Scared? Of me?" *Oh no.*

"Not of you, but of what's going to happen between you. He doesn't want to go home."

I frowned. "Where are you?"

"In Bristol."

Bristol? *Shit.*

"Look, Damian. He's very fragile, as you already know. He's not going to go home with the way he left things. Josh doesn't just feel embarrassment and sadness, like people without his disorder would in this situation. For him it's humiliation and grief."

"I know." I'd read up on all I could find. I knew that. I also knew that impulsive reactions weren't just the cutting, but also running away. Like he'd apparently done now.

"I think you should come here and talk to him. Just tell him how sorry you are, that you didn't mean it. If he hears it from you directly, I'm sure it will soothe him quite a lot."

I swallowed again.

Head down to Bristol?

"Do you have half-term too? The next week off?"

"Yeah."

"Then how about I buy a train ticket for you for tomorrow morning? I'll come pick you up at the train station when you get here."

There wasn't even something to think about. "Okay." I needed to talk to Josh, and if I had to go down to Bristol to do it, I would. "Okay."

"Great." Her voice rose a bit, which told me she was happy about my decision.

If she was happy, surely that would mean Josh would be too, right? He'd run away, but if I grovelled and apologised profusely—and told him about my past, so he'd know exactly what I had to deal with once a year—then surely he would come back?

∼

I BROUGHT school books on the train to read. It might be half-term, but getting ahead in my reading would only be a plus.

When I finally arrived at the station in Bristol, Angelina waited for me just outside. She was easy enough to spot, with her blond hair cut into a sharp middle-length bob.

I grimaced at the thought. The only reason I even knew what the cut was called was because of Chloe. She'd been obsessed with it a few years ago, always getting hers cut so it wouldn't grow out.

"Hey, Damian." She smiled at me and I managed a nervous one in return. "My car's this way."

I followed her, all the while toying with the strap of my bag. I didn't know how Josh would react to seeing me and I didn't exactly look forward to the conversation we needed to have.

"Josh went out with his cousin last night, so he spent the night with him." Angelina started the car and drove swiftly out of the parking space. "Cooper has a bad habit of getting smashed out of his mind every weekend, so I'm not sure they even made it home. Josh has a tendency to drink a lot, too."

"Alcohol abuse is common impulsive behaviour in borderliners," I said.

She cast me a wry look as she stopped for a red light. "You've done your research."

"Of course. I needed to know what to look out for and what not to do." I stared out the window. "Obviously I didn't take into equation what happens around this time in October."

"What happens around this time in October?"

"Everything goes to shit." I didn't want to share it with anyone, but I knew I had to with Josh. Josh had to understand what always went through my head at these particular dates every year. I didn't want yesterday to ever repeat itself again. "I lived with my uncle and aunt. There's... a good reason for that."

She didn't prod more into it.

She soon parked the car. "Cooper's flat is on the second floor." She pointed out the house we were parked in front of. "If Cooper made it home last night, tell him he can come with me. We'll buy some food for us while you and Josh talk."

I left my bag in the car and headed upstairs.

I knocked on the door and waited anxiously for it to open.

It took a while, and I was just about to knock again, when Josh stood in front of me.

He blinked. "Damian?"

"Hey." Something washed over me once I laid eyes on him. Affection, relief, nervousness. A bundle of mixed feelings I didn't know how to separate. "Can I come in?"

He stepped out of the way.

"Is your cousin home?"

He nodded.

"Your mum says he can go with her to buy food, while we talk."

Josh went into the room to our left, and I heard muffled voices, before two pair of footsteps announced their arrival.

I couldn't help but stare at his cousin when he emerged, because he looked a lot like Josh. His hair was a bit longer, and a lot more ruffled. His bare arms were smooth, eyes red and peering at me, and they were blue, instead of Josh's green ones. There were also differences in their facial built, which was noticeable to me now, but from a distance they would've looked like twins.

"Bloody hell. I fell asleep with my contacts in," Cooper muttered. He padded past me in nothing but low-hanging joggers and into what I assumed was the bathroom.

"He's not a morning person," Josh excused his cousin's lack of greeting.

It didn't matter. He wasn't the one I was here to see.

We stood there, a bit awkwardly, while Cooper got ready in the bathroom. We kept shooting glances at each other, but we both looked away when we were caught at it. It was like we were back in lower secondary school.

"You better make up pretty darn good," Cooper muttered as he came out of the bathroom again. He was dressed more properly now and he also wore glasses. "If you want to shag, feel free to use my bed."

He put on trainers, grabbed a jacket, and then slammed the door after himself.

This was the person I'd been jealous off back when Josh and I had just met? "So that was Cooper." I turned back to Josh.

"Yeah." Josh's arms folded tightly in front of him. "He's... special. But he's got his reasons like the rest of us do."

I cleared my throat. "About that... what happened yesterday. I've got my reasons."

His Adam's apple bobbed furiously. "You don't want me anymore, do you?"

"Don't jump to conclusions, Josh. I do. I wouldn't

be here if I didn't." I stepped closer to him, put a hand on his shoulder, and steered him over to the sofa.

He sank down and I sat on the arm of it, because I couldn't sit close to him when I told him about my past.

"You know I've been real busy with coursework this month. I've been so busy I didn't realise what month it was, so I haven't been able to prepare myself for the date. And I saw it yesterday and I realised it was only four days until *the day*, and I have a hard enough time dealing when I know it's coming —so I didn't do so well when I realised it yesterday. And you came in and you touched me, and I just reacted like I've done every other year. I don't like being touched when I'm remembering or thinking about what happened."

He sat quietly, eyes on me, expectant. His hands were still folded in his lap and I noticed he was only in a T-shirt—and that both his arms were bandaged. They hadn't been for the last week, so that had to have happened yesterday.

I felt immensely guilty. I tried my best not to upset him, to show him affection and be with him, and I'd messed it up. I'd made him hurt himself—it was because of *me*.

"You're not the only one who's got scars."

He blinked. "You cut yourself too?"

"No." I scratched a hand over my chest. "I've only got the one. And I didn't do it to myself."

His eyebrows drew together in a frown. "Someone hurt you?"

I bit down on my lip. "Someone tried to kill me."

His eyes widened in surprise.

"It's the kind of situation that only ever happens in films—but it happened to me in real life." Whenever I talked about it I always felt phantom pains in my scar. Now was no exception.

"Was it someone you knew?" He was sitting on the edge of the sofa now.

I cast around for something to look at that wasn't him. "My mother."

A short gasp escaped him, drawing my focus back to him. "Why? Or no, you don't have to tell me why. It's probably too horrible to want to talk about."

I shrugged. "Don't really know why. I was the only one who survived."

"Of the two of you?"

"Of the five of us." His eyes grew wide again. I continued speaking before he could ask. "My dad and my two younger sisters died. Then my mother killed herself." He was getting teary now. "Don't cry. It's the way it is. Nothing can be changed. I haven't cried in years."

"When did it happen?" Despite my words, a few tears escaped.

"When I was twelve." I scratched at my chest again. I didn't even know I'd been doing it until I saw his attention drawn to it.

"Where's your scar? Is it there?"

"On my chest, yeah."

"Can I see it?" He seemed to be strangely fascinated.

I hesitated.

That would mean taking my clothes off.

"I don't like being touched there. I don't like anyone seeing it. I don't like to take my clothes off."

He stood up and came to stand in front of me. His hands slid to the back of my neck to tangle in the hair in my nape. "Two and a half months. That's how long we've known each other. That's how long we've been together. Maybe not officially, but I like to think we've been together since the day we met. Once I saw you, there could never be anyone else."

I stared up into his eyes.

He wet his lips nervously. "I'm in love with you. I *love* you."

"I'm sorry for pushing you." I grabbed a hold of his waist and pulled him closer to me. I spread my knees to accommodate him in closer, and his arms wrapped around my shoulders as I leant my head against his chest. "I can't stand to be touched. I never got affection when I was little, and afterwards... I couldn't stand for anyone to be close to me, so Ray and Claire kept their distance. You're the only one I've ever been able to be close to. But two days ago... I just couldn't deal, knowing the date was too close and you showing up then was unfortunate. I didn't mean to push you. I never should've done that."

His hands carded through my hair. He bent over slightly so his lips rested against the top of my head. "I don't know what your experience was like for you, but I know mine. I can't control my emotions at all and I think you do a great job of it. The other day excluded, obviously."

I closed my eyes and simply enjoyed the feel of him against me. I had him back. He wasn't leaving me.

He loves me.

I should say it too, because I did. I did so much, but I couldn't find the voice to do so. The words stuck in my throat.

I was the shittiest person alive to not say the words back—and he was the person that needed to hear those kinds of words the most.

I pulled back, hands slipping from around him to toy with the hem of my jumper. "I don't want to take it off. But I could pull it up."

Confusion flitted over his face, and I pulled both the jumper and my T-shirt up before he realised what I was going on about.

His attention zeroed in on my chest. I could see how his gaze started up at my shoulder, then followed the thick scar down across to my waist.

"Just one scar," I said, refusing to look down at myself. "But it's a big one."

"Oh Jesus." His hands fluttered, one in front of his mouth, the other towards me.

I sucked my stomach in, an unconscious move to get further away, but his hand touched my skin, his fingers felt over the roughness of the scar. Goosebumps erupted, and they weren't the good kind.

He pulled away after a while and I let my clothes fall back into place. We looked at each other.

"I'm sorry I ran away," he whispered. "I should've stayed. Should've let you have some space, then asked you what was wrong. I can't believe you came all the way here just to tell me this."

"I didn't come just to tell you, Josh. I came to make you come back home with me."

That brought the tears back. "You want to still be with me?"

"Yeah. More than anything else." I couldn't imagine being without him. The previous day had been pure hell. "Please come back."

He all but threw himself around my neck.

"I'll take that as a yes."

"I'll be here for as long as you'll have me."

"It's going to be for a great length of time then."

Two and a half months together, and I already knew that.

CHAPTER 28

JOSH

"Get down on your hands and knees and brace your hands against the wall." The voice was cold, yet somehow it vibrated excitement.

I was shivering and tears were falling freely down my cheeks. I didn't fight him though. I never did. I'd learned it was for the best. He'd trained me well.

I glanced over my shoulder. His fly was already undone, showing off what was hiding underneath. I felt the bile rise, even more so when he removed the belt from the loops and almost lovingly ran his hands over the leather.

His eyes lifted to look at me. "This is your own fault, Joshua. Remember that."

I turned back to face the wall. I couldn't watch him. I squeezed my eyes shut and bit down on my lower lip. I *didn't want to make a sound when he whipped me, but I knew I would. I always did.*

I jerked forward when the leather whipped across my back with all the force he could muster. All my pretences of not making a sound were lost in the pain of it.

"*N*O!" I wrestled with what held me down, with what kept me trapped. I screamed and screamed and screamed. I couldn't stop. I couldn't take more of his abuse, neither the physical nor the sexual. I just wanted to *die*.

"Josh!"

Death would be a relief. Death would be peaceful. No one could hurt me when I was dead.

"Josh!"

Someone shook me, rather roughly.

Reality started to come back.

I was drenched in sweat, the sheets were tangled around me, and a warm, strong hand was on my shoulder.

"Get it off me, get it off me, get it off of me!" I clawed at my shirt. I was soaked in my own sweat.

I think he helped me out of it. He must've, because I couldn't possibly have managed it on my own. But the cool air soon hit my heated skin, drying the sweat that clung to me.

I drew my knees up under me, buried my face in the duvet, and wrapped my arms over my head. I rocked, back and forth, while I cried.

"Do you want us to do anything, D?"

It was Silver's voice.

I hadn't even realised he was in the room. With the plural, I suspected Kian was there as well, but I couldn't unfold myself. I couldn't look at them.

All I could do was rock back and forth and let it all out. All the tears, all the sadness, all the bitterness of everything I'd lost. All the anger at being such a mess, with a severe brain damage disguised as a mental disorder.

"I don't know." Damian's voice shook. If I'd been screaming as loud as I thought I'd been, I must've scared him to death.

"You want me to call Vincent?"

"No, no. It'll be fine. I've got it. Thanks though."

"Don't hesitate to tell me if you change your mind. If he doesn't calm down." I heard two pairs of footsteps leave. Kian whispered something right before the door shut, but I didn't catch it.

"Hey, Josh." Damian rubbed my back. "It was just a dream."

I drew in several shaky breaths.

"Want to lie back down with me?" He carefully pried my arms away from around my head, and I went willingly as he had to practically wrestle me back into a stretched out position.

He pulled his duvet over both of us.

It was warm, but not soaked in sweat like mine was. My upper body was still completely bare, and his hand stroked my upper arm and shoulder now as I rested against him, my cheek on his chest.

"Don't you ever have nightmares?" His past was just as horrible as mine. Maybe even more so, because he'd lost everyone close to him.

"I used to. Not so much anymore." He gripped my shoulder now. Clearly the subject wasn't one he was comfortable in. "When I do have them, it's not like yours. I don't wake up screaming. I hardly ever wake up at all. I've got the nightmare, and it feels real, but most of the time I can't wake up. And it just phases into another dream or another nightmare. Most of the times I can't even remember having it when I do wake up."

"That must be nice." I wish I could have a nightmare without waking up like I just had. Without the need to hurt myself, or kill myself, or cut myself. "I wish I didn't have to remember."

He hugged me tight, but he didn't say anything. He never did when there was nothing to say. Because there wasn't anything that could be done.

I would never forget. I would always struggle

with what had been done to me for those ten years. I'd been abused for seven years longer than I'd been free of it. The first five years I couldn't even remember.

"Stop thinking." Damian pushed me away from him, and then he rolled onto his side so we were facing each other. I couldn't see him properly in the darkened room, but I could see his shadows. We were almost nose to nose.

"Sometimes I think I wouldn't even be here if it wasn't for you," I admitted in a low voice. "If I'd just had Mum... I don't think I could've been strong enough. But I've got you and you're all mine, and I don't want to lose that."

"You won't." He stroked my cheek. "You won't lose me. I promise."

"Even if I run away again? Even if I'm hospitalised indefinitely? Even if I never get better?"

"Even then."

My chest squeezed with an immense feeling of love towards him. "What made you fall for me?"

He hesitated only briefly. "I honestly don't know. There was a connection. You know, I told you, Silver referred to us as scarred souls. Might be that. We don't share the same experiences, but we're both scarred, both on the inside and the outside, and maybe I just immediately felt that pull towards you that told me we were alike. That we could be good. Great, even."

"I think you're great. Me, not so much." I curled one hand under my pillow. The other one rested on the small space in-between our bodies.

"I think you are." He flicked a piece of fringe away from my forehead and leaned in to kiss it. "I know we're not passionate, but I like what we have. It's relaxing, it's a good feeling to know I've got someone who cares for me just as deeply as I care for them."

He hadn't said the L-word back to me the other day, back in Bristol. It had bothered me, it still did, but this soothed that hurt. I'd said I loved him, and if he felt as deeply for me as I did for him... then he had to love me.

"You mentioned once that you'd been in therapy too. I've never heard you say you went to a session though."

"I usually don't have to, but I did set up an appointment for the end of the week. I don't deal well at this time of year. It's all so close, you know? Ray and Claire always want to visit the graves and I just... I don't deal with it well."

He dealt better than me. But I suppose that didn't mean much. Everyone dealt with their issues better than I did. It wasn't exactly a great feat to accomplish.

"I'm so sorry for what happened to you." It was a horrible thing for anyone to experience.

"I'm so sorry for what happened to *you*. You have a harder time dealing with your past than I have. You're not doing okay. I nearly had a heart attack when I heard you scream. Silver and Kian came barging in here too. It was…" He searched for the word, but he didn't find it.

"I'm terrified of him," I whispered. "The times he was gentle, it was bearable. My body liked it. But mostly he wasn't. He liked seeing me in pain. And I'm just so terrified." I couldn't even describe what it'd been like for all those years. "When I tried to kill myself, I *really* tried. I wanted to die.

"When I woke up in hospital I was gutted. I thought I would be going right back to what I'd tried to escape. Mum was there. I broke down on her. I told her everything. I still remember the look on her face. She'd been worried before I opened my mouth and I remember wondering why she was, because she'd never bothered with me. Then when I told her… she was raging. She didn't question me. She believed me instantly. And she called the police. They arrested him right there, in the hospital. I remember them escorting him out of my room. I remember meeting his eyes... they promised me that if he ever got his hands on me again, I would regret ever opening my mouth."

Damian's arm slid over my waist. It felt good having it there, all warm and safe. "He won't get his hands on you again. He's in prison."

"But he'll get out."

"You'll be a grown man by then. Of no interest to him."

"He's got eight years to plan his revenge. It's my fault he's in prison. Trust me, I'm going to be of a lot of interest to him." I trembled by the simple thought of it.

"He's not going to get near you. Everyone'll make sure of that." His arm tightened around me, drawing me in closer to him. "He went to prison once for hurting you. He's not going to risk it again, for sure."

I wasn't so sure.

Surely, in his mind, I'd ruined his life.

But I didn't want to think about it anymore.

"Remember you asked me if my mum knew your boss?"

He looked at me, recognising the change in subject for what it was. "Yeah."

"Turns out they *do* know each more. More than that, in fact."

"What'd you mean?"

"They're together. Mum told me the day before yesterday. She was going to tell me Friday, but well… the way she found me, I wasn't fit for a talk. So she told me the day after, when we went out to eat, just the two of us." I buried my face against his neck. "My mum's a lesbian."

He chuckled. "I'm pretty sure she's not. She was married to a bloke, after all."

It hadn't been much of a marriage. She'd never been home. He'd been busy with me. "And she did get me with someone."

"Do you know your father?"

I shook my head. "It was a drunken one-night-stand. She can't even remember what he looked like."

"How can someone sleep with someone and not remember them the day after?"

It was my turn to chuckle.

I threw my own arm around him. "Because most people are a lot more easy-going when it comes to sex than you are. I've been with blokes I couldn't remember before. It's all part of heavy drinking. You let loose, you pull, then you sober up and can't remember shit. Everyone's got at least one of those. Everyone who likes to party and have sex, anyway."

He was silent for a moment, thinking. "Do you miss it?"

"What?"

"Sex."

"Uh. Actually, no. Not really."

"You sure about that?"

"Sex is good when it's done right." I couldn't say it wasn't, because that would be a lie. "But all my life's been about it, and like you've said to me, this is nice. Being close to someone without that, it's actually quite relaxing. I'm enjoying it. I don't need sex. Especially now I know you don't want it with anyone, that it's not just with me you're against it."

"I'm not against sex. I just don't want to have it myself. I'm fine with others having it, as long as I don't get it shoved in my face."

"You never want to have sex?" I wasn't sure how I felt about it. It didn't outright bother me, but at the same time, wasn't sex important for intimacy?

"Not really, no."

"But you still want to be with me? Like a proper relationship? You and me, exclusive?"

"Yeah, of course."

"But without the sex?"

He nodded. It was awkward, with my head pressed against his neck, so his chin hit the top of my head, but I got it.

"If that's something you can live with?" he asked

eventually, once it was clear I wasn't going to say anything else.

"I… I think it is. Yeah." As long as I had him, what more would I need?

"Let me know if that changes." He whispered it against my hair. "If it does, we could try to work something out. I guess."

My turn to nod awkwardly. "I don't foresee it anytime soon. This whole no sex situation is actually rather nice." He chuckled. "Though, I honestly can't be held accountable for my body's reactions. Morning wood's quite common, I'm just saying."

"I think I'll survive, that."

Just like that, my nightmare was forgotten. How could I honestly keep thinking about that hell when I had this, here, right now?

I wouldn't say the ten years had been worth it, but surviving my suicide attempt definitely was.

OCTOBER 21ST

Today hasn't been a good day. Today was **the** day.

Damian was quiet and far-away all day. I let him be. I didn't want to try to get close to him, only to be pushed away again.

I understand him now, I do. But even if I do understand, I don't want to test the theory out if he were to push me away again.

He went with his uncle and aunt to visits his family's graves.

He didn't ask me to accompany him.

It hurt, of course it did, but I try my best not to let it get to me. This is his tragedy, not something I should take personally.

I'm trying my best to be there for him, all quiet and supportive, without getting too close to him.

I think he appreciates it.

I'm not sure if it's the quiet and supportiveness he appreciates or the fact that I'm trying not to get close to him that does it. But anyway.

I'll take the appreciation where I can.

OCTOBER 26TH

Things have settled down again.

Before, I used to be a roller coaster of emotions every single day. But nowadays, I feel more evened out. I'm not saying I'm not feeling like a roller coaster anymore, because I am, it's just slowed down.

A slow-motion roller coaster.

He spent the week of half-term with me. He didn't even open a single book. It was just the two of us, together—and Silver and Kian, of course. Kian's staying over almost as often as I am nowadays.

It's nice. We've all got real close. They're my real friends.

I love all three of them, I really do.

NOVEMBER 3RD

Dinner with mum and Harriet was… interesting.

Harriet didn't bring her nephew, like mum had initially said she would. Apparently he backed out? Without even telling her.

I don't know Harriet, so I can't read her, but I'm pretty sure it did upset her. She was quiet through the entire dinner, and that's not at all like I've experienced her at the Café. There she's all smiles.

Not so much tonight.

But I understand.

She was let down.

Besides that downer, mum seemed happy. I'd go so far as to say she looked in love. They sure seemed to have chemistry, if I was to judge by the looks and the small smiles they exchanged throughout the entire dinner.

It's nice.

Mum's getting on with her life, as she should. She shouldn't have to dwell on Andrew anymore. She's divorced him and he's out of both of our lives.

Well, not quite. We still have to live with the after effects of what he's done.

But we're moving on.

NOVEMBER 27TH

Coursework's kicking my arse.

The first few weeks it was okay, because it was all stuff I'd been through the year before. But now... now we're at the stuff I didn't get to go through because I was hospitalised.

Damian helps me study whenever he doesn't have to study himself. That helps, because he's real smart. He finished his A-levels with top grades, after all, and he's still getting top grades now he's in medical school. Not that I'm jealous or anything. I just feel real dumb sometimes.

I know he doesn't mean to, but sometimes I ask questions and he looks at me like I'm mental. And he answers like it's the most obvious thing in the world. I guess for him it is, because he's so bloody smart.

But I'm not. I'm not smart. I've never given a shit about coursework. It didn't use to be part of my future. My future had been to be dead.

And now that it's not, I actually have to try my best at this. I still don't know what I want to do afterwards, but I want to have decent grades so I'll have a good chance at getting into university later. If that's what I figure out I want, anyway.

I have no idea what I want. He does.

Now that I'm jealous of.

CHAPTER 29

JOSH

I asked Mal to go to the cinema with me.

Damian worked late and Mal looked worse than ever, so I figured why not. I'd tried since college started to make friends with him. I wasn't sure I'd succeeded. He did sit with me at lunch, but that was it.

He did, however, say yes to go to the cinema with me.

"You can pick the film," he said once we were there. "I don't care what we watch."

I picked an action-comedy. It was the one that looked most decent. We both got something to drink, and I got popcorn. Mal insisted he didn't want anything else. I didn't press.

I chuckled several times throughout the movie. At

a couple of points I even had to laugh. But I noticed that Mal didn't. Not even once.

It was dark out when we exited the cinema.

We headed the same way.

I wasn't even sure where Mal lived, but I figured he knew where he was going. I searched for something to say as we walked along the pavement. Cars drove past us in quick succession.

I jumped in surprise when a small, shaking hand slid into mine.

I looked at Mal, but he had his head bowed.

"Please don't hate me," he whispered.

"Why would I hate you?"

"I can't do it anymore." Then his hand slipped from mine, he pushed me hard, right in the middle of my chest and he threw himself into the road.

It all happened in slow motion.

Mal was smaller and slighter than me—yet he pushed me with quite a bit of force.

I stumbled backwards, lost my balance and crashed to the pavement, while Mal... Mal threw himself right out into the street. Lights illumined him for a second, but the car was going too fast, and Mal stood his ground and there was a sound I couldn't even describe when the front of the car connected with Mal's body.

"NO! MAL! *NO!*"

I pushed myself up onto my knees, saw a body crumple to the ground, heard the noises from all the cars that'd been forced to stop.

And I screamed.

I screamed and screamed and screamed.

I couldn't stop—because Mal wasn't moving. There was something dark around his head, I could see a few ruffled blond strands sticking out from the hood.

Blood.

Blood pooled around him.

"No, no, no, *NO!*" I bent down, over my knees, and tucked my head against them.

And all the while I couldn't stop screaming.

CHAPTER 30

DAMIAN

"Closing at eleven is ridiculously late," Harriet said.

I wiped down the counter, nodding my agreement to it.

"It's winter now, it gets dark early. I'm thinking we could start closing maybe eight or nine? It's not like we earn enough from nine to eleven that it makes a difference. Kind of more expensive, you know, with having to pay someone to be here for that long when there's hardly any people."

I nodded my agreement again.

She leant against the counter. She had a notebook in front of her and she scribbled something in it.

"I think we should start new hours come Monday.

It's almost ten now and there's no one here." She turned and motioned around the Café, just to emphasise her point.

I got it.

But just as she finished talking, the doorbell rang, signalling customers.

Except it wasn't. It was Angelina.

I turned back to wiping down the counter, figuring she was there for Harriet, like she tended to be nowadays.

"Hey, you." Harriet went around the counter to greet her. "What a lovely surprise. I didn't know we were seeing each other today."

"We're not." Angelina's voice was low, almost sad. It brought my attention to her. "I'm sorry, love, but I'm not here for you."

Harriet frowned at the back of her head as Angelina turned to me.

My chest squeezed in fearful anticipation. "Just say it." I didn't want her to hesitate, or come with a long story about what had happened. "Whatever it is, just say it."

"Josh is in the hospital. He's been hospitalised."

My breath hitched. "Is he all right?" Obviously he wasn't, else he wouldn't have been hospitalised.

She shook her head. "He is, physically. But his

friend…" She cleared her throat. "His friend just killed himself."

"Which friend?" My voice shook. Josh didn't have many friends, and those he had… they were my friends too. Kind of, anyway. He was closer to Spencer and Leslie than I'd ever been.

She pinched the bridge of his nose. "His name's Mal. Was Mal, I suppose is the better term."

Mal? The troubled one from college—and from Josh's group therapy. "What happened?"

"He jumped in front of a car. He was dead before the EMTs arrived. Might even have died on impact."

"And Josh saw it all?" I didn't even know he hung out with Mal once school was over.

Angelina nodded. She bit her lip. "He wouldn't stop screaming. They sedated him, then hospitalised him." She sighed. "He's been doing so well lately. I'm afraid this is going to put him back on square one again."

"How long's he going to be in the hospital?" I wanted to see him. I *needed* to see him.

"For now, only for the night. But he's sedated now, he's sleeping. A psychiatrist will be to see him tomorrow, and then he or she will deem him fit, or not, to be discharged."

"And if not?"

"Then he'll be sectioned."

Silence fell between us. She had no more to say, and I didn't know what to say.

Harriet glanced between us. "All right, we're closing up."

"You don't have to." Angelina turned back to her. "We can't see him tonight anyway."

"We still can't work now." Harriet strode over to lock the door. "I wouldn't expect Damian to work after what he's just found out. And I can't work and be here for you at the same time."

I went to change and get my shoulder bag while Harriet turned everything off.

"I'll fix everything tomorrow morning," she told me when I eyed everything that was part of the closing routine. "Don't think about it."

"Do you want to come with us?" Angelina's eyes rested on me.

I shook my head. "No, I'll—I'm just going to go home."

I walked home in a stupor. Josh wouldn't be coming home tonight. He was in hospital, drugged. Drugged because something had happened he hadn't been able to deal with.

Angelina had said he wouldn't stop screaming. If it had been anything like that night after we'd got back from Bristol... He'd scared me to death that night, waking up screaming like he had.

But I'd been there then, and I'd managed to soothe him. He'd been in a good mood once we fell back asleep.

I hated that I hadn't been there for him now. That he'd been all alone while his friend, or someone he'd tried very hard to make his friend, had voluntarily jumped in front of a car.

"You're home early, mate." Silver was on the sofa when I got home, and Kian was straddling with his lap. Silver had his hands under Kian's tight shirt, while Kian's were buried down Silver's jeans.

Normally I would've looked away the minute I spotted the compromising position, but now I couldn't. It wasn't them I was seeing anyway, not really.

What did it matter that they were fondling each other on the sofa now, anyway?

"Hey." Silver slowly pulled his hands back so Kian's shirt fell down to cover his smooth, pale skin.

Kian extracted his own hands from Silver's jeans, and even buttoned them up before he looked at me.

They were both worried.

"Josh's in hospital."

"Hospital?" Kian frowned. "He left a few hours ago to go to the cinema."

"And now he's in hospital." I dropped my shoulder bag without a care to what might happen to it, then I sat down on the other sofa. "The one he went to the cinema with—he killed himself." At least I assumed Mal had gone with him to the cinema. I couldn't imagine Josh going alone.

"Shit." Silver scooted out from under Kian, closer to me. "Is Josh all right? Have you been to see him?"

I shook my head. I could see the horror on both their faces at it, and realised they might take that as an answer to the first question. "Angelina said Josh was all right physically, but they had to sedate him because he wouldn't stop screaming. He's not doing well mentally, and I'm scared for tomorrow."

"Why?"

"Because I don't know what it'll be like when I go to see him. He hasn't been hospitalised since we met, so I don't know how bad it's going to be."

I wanted to see him, I really did, but at the same time I dreaded it. If they'd had to sedate him... it must've been real bad.

I stood from the sofa again. "I'm going to bed." The quicker I could sleep, the quicker the morning would come, with whatever it would bring.

~

I ARRIVED at the hospital the minute visitors were allowed.

When I met up with Angelina, I instantly knew something was wrong. She stood with her head in her hands, and she nodded ferociously at something a doctor said to her.

I stayed back until she'd finished speaking to him, since it wasn't a conversation I was privy too.

But the moment the doctor walked off, I was besides her.

"What's wrong?" Something was. I could tell. My chest squeezed, my stomach churned.

Her hands fell away from her face and when she turned to me, she'd pulled herself together. "They had to sedate him again. He woke up and started hurting himself. There's no doubt he's being sectioned now, but they can't start a treatment plan until he's awake and calm."

Something squeezed tighter around my chest. "I can't see him?" He was sedated. Of course I couldn't see him.

Or if I could, I wouldn't be able to talk to him.

She shook her head sadly. "All we can do is wait until he's calm enough for them to get anywhere with him."

"Do they have, like, an estimated timeline or something?"

"No. He might be just as distraught when he wakes up the next time. They didn't even get to tell him why they'd sedated him in the first time. The doctor said he'd been so set on hurting himself. All they could do was sedate him again." She smoothed her hair down. It struck me as a nervous gesture and not one of vanity. "This is bad. He hasn't been so bad in two years. He was after he woke up from his suicide attempt. But he got help then."

"How long was he sectioned for then?" Josh hadn't told me much about his hospitalisation. Most of our conversation about his past and disorder were about his stepfather.

"Three months."

Three months?

"In a locked ward. People on the locked wards are sicker than the people admitted to the open ones. They need more vigorous help. He's going to be admitted to a locked ward this time too."

A locked ward. "Does that mean I don't get to see him?"

"Family and friends are involved in the treatment, if the patient wishes it. I'm sure he'll want you involved. You are very important to him."

Hearing that warmed me.

"There's nothing I can do here now. I was going to meet Harriet at the Café. Do you want to come?"

"Yeah, okay." It wasn't like I had anything else to do now I wouldn't be able to see Josh. All I'd wanted was to see him—and I wouldn't be able to.

And I had no idea when I would be able to see him again.

CHAPTER 31

DAMIAN

I didn't know why I stood hesitantly outside the door.

Just inside it, he waited for me.

And I was outside, not daring to open the bloody door.

Man up. You haven't seen him in a week.

I went inside, but stopped again once I was over the threshold.

Josh sat on the bed, legs crossed. His head lifted slowly to look at me. His eyes were sad, dejected almost. It was uncanny how well I could read Josh, whereas with most other people I didn't have a clue what they were thinking or feeling.

"Hey," I said.

"Hey." His voice was low. His eyes searched mine.

It was good to see him again. He was alive, he seemed to be well, and it was just so *bloody good*.

I strode over the floor to him and he met me at the edge of the bed. His arms went around my neck, while mine wrapped around his torso.

"You're here," he muttered against my neck. "You're really here."

"I've missed you." He was all warm, hard, male body. I'd never thought I'd ever miss feeling someone like this, but I'd missed him like mad. "I've missed you so much."

He was in a T-shirt and his arms were free of gauze. I could feel the rough texture of his scars against the skin on my neck.

We didn't have anything to say to each other just then.

Instead we held on tight, like we were both afraid to let go.

I was; I was afraid to let him go.

"I brought your journal." I handed the leather-bound book to him once we took a step back from each other. "You've been without it for a week. Figured you'd go mental without it." I didn't realise before the words were out that it was a poor choice of them. He was sectioned in a psychiatric ward, after all.

He didn't seem to take notice of my words though. All he had eyes for was the journal. He stroked the leather lovingly and unbound the string to look through the pages within.

"Thank you." He smiled up at me once he'd closed it again. "I've been itching to write. I don't feel right writing on random paper. I need the journal for it."

We sat down on the edge of his bed. I slid one arm around his waist. It seemed I couldn't keep my hands off him. He didn't mind though, since he leaned into me willingly.

"How are things?"

"The same. You know, busy with course-work, working a few night a week." Life had moved on even if he hadn't been there. "I walked in on Silver and Kian in an extremely compromising position the other day. It was beyond mortifying."

That brought a chuckle from him. "Were they naked?"

"Yeah."

"Were they shagging?"

"Yeah." My cheeks burned. I must've been even redder when I'd actually walked in on them though. It truly had been mortifying. It couldn't be explained.

"They're very… passionate."

"If that's what you want to call it." They shared a flat with someone else. They should be more careful.

"What would you call it?"

"Them being slags?"

Another chuckled escaped him. "They're in an exclusive, committed relationship. I don't think that qualifies them as slags."

Maybe so. It didn't really matter. "They miss you. They wanted me to tell you that."

"I miss them too." He leaned his head on my shoulder.

"Spencer and Leslie say hi too." Ever since Josh had befriended them, and I still wasn't quite clear on just how he'd managed that, they'd started talking more to me too.

"That's nice. Tell them I'm good." He hung his head.

"Are you though?" I eyed him wryly.

"Hmm?"

"Doing good?"

I instantly regretted asking it, because his whole demeanour changed. His shoulders hunched and the small smile he'd had fell away. But at the same time I needed to know.

"Right now, when you're here, I am."

"But when I'm not here, you're not?"

He shook his head slowly. "I can't stop seeing it. Seeing Mal, jumping in front of that car. It wasn't just random, you know. He pushed me first, so hard I fell. So I couldn't stop him. Then he did it. I can't stop hearing the sound when the car hit him. It was a horrendous sound. And then he was just lying there in the street."

I wrapped my arm around his shoulders.

He leaned into me.

"His funeral's today. I can't go, because I'm in here."

"Can't they let you go to it? I mean, it's a funeral. You're only going to have one chance at going to it."

"I don't think I can anyway. Like, mentally I don't think I can handle it."

I squeezed him tight.

"I can't believe he did it. Like that. He just threw himself out into the street. He didn't even hesitate." He huddled against me. "He asked me to please don't hate him. Said he couldn't do it anymore. Then he pushed me and jumped right in front of an oncoming car."

I'd read that about one in ten people with borderline personality disorder committed suicide. Josh had said Mal shared the same diagnosis as him, and he'd been part of those statistics.

Josh had tried to kill himself once, and he cut

himself, but I could only hope he wouldn't be part of the statistics as well.

I didn't know what to say to make him feel better. Quoting statistics sure wouldn't do anything. It would likely make him feel worse, considering he had the disorder too. I didn't want to say anything that could compromise his rather calm mood right now.

"How's the last week been for you?" I hadn't seen or spoken to him all week. I'd hardly even talked to Angelina. I hadn't seen the point. I didn't want updates from her. I wanted them from Josh directly.

"Chaotic," was all he said, and I could imagine that that was exactly what it had been like. "It's all so chaotic. People don't like me here, I know it. I'm calm one moment, then suddenly I'm raging and I don't even know why." He wrung his hands together. "I think I've been doing well for the past half a year. Before I met you, too, except when it came to the trial and all that. And after we met… I think I've been good. But now I'm back to how I used to be before and it's just… it's chaos."

"That's why you're here. So they can help you. And I'm sure they like you. Everyone's who's in here is here to get help or they're here to give help."

He pulled away from me, eyes dark and hooded when he lifted his head. "I keep doubting you."

"Me? Why?"

"Because you're not here."

"I haven't been allowed to be here." It hurt to hear. I knew it was all part of being him though, of being borderline. I knew he couldn't help it. But it chafed.

"I want you to from now on. I told them I wanted my mum involved—and you."

"I want to be." Being involved with his treatment wouldn't just be good for him, but also for me and for us. It would make me understand him better, instead of relying on everything I'd read.

I knew not all of it would be relevant to Josh and there was more to him than what was written on sites with general information about being borderline.

He scooted back in close to me. "I love you so much."

I stared into his eyes. They were big and sincere. "I do too." I still couldn't say the word. I leaned in to kiss him, to hopefully make up for the fact that I hadn't.

He returned it. He even cupped his hand around my neck.

I liked it when he did that.

He pulled back when I ran my fingers over both of his forearms. He licked his lips and cast his eyes down. "Ugly, right?"

I shook my head. "Nothing about you is ugly."

He snorted. He didn't believe it. But it *was* true. Yes, his arms were all scars, and I would've preferred for him not to have to have that reminder for the rest of his life. But at the same time, the cutting was what had helped him through all the years of abuse. They were a part of him, they'd been of help to him, they were his history.

I couldn't find anything ugly about that.

"I have to go to group therapy soon." He leaned his forehead against my temple. "It's all about being active here. Group therapy, group activities, single therapy, single activities. I've started working out. Apparently that can help. As well as proper sleep, a healthy diet, and they say I should stop drinking."

"That's probably wise." I didn't drink myself, but I'd seen enough to know that people did stupid shit when they were smashed. And with him being borderline and the impulsiveness that came with that... drinking wasn't such a good idea. "I have to get to work soon, too."

"Will you come back tomorrow?"

"Of course I will." I stroked his back, feeling the ridges in his spine. I hoped his new healthy diet and exercise would help him gain some weight, because he was definitely too thin. "I'll miss you."

That brought forth a smile. "I'll miss you too." He

wrapped both arms around my neck in a tight hug. "Please don't give up on me," he whispered.

"I won't. I won't ever do that." Maybe that wasn't the best promise to make, considering everything, but I knew it was true. He was it for me. He was the only person who'd ever drawn my interest. He was the only person who'd ever got close to me. "Just come back."

"I will. I just have to get better first."

DECEMBER 10TH

Someone tried to kill themselves today.

There were threats, yelling, people running this way and that. It was chaos. And chaos in my surroundings definitely didn't help the chaos in my mind.

So I went to my room and curled up on my bed. It's a nice coping mechanism when I haven't got a razor nearby. It's even a healthy one, I'd say.

My therapist here thought so anyway. Because when things had calmed, they came around to talk to everyone. Ask us if we were okay after what had happened, if we needed something, anything.

I think the people here are real nice. My psychiatrist here isn't Vincent, but I feel like they can help me anyway. I'm calmer than I was when I came here.

I want to make sense of the chaos in my head. I think they're fully equipped to help with that.

DECEMBER 22ND

I messed up. The thought of spending Christmas away from everyone is unbearable. I messed up so bad.

Why do I always do this? Why do I ruin everything? Why do I have to be me? I don't want to be me. I don't want to be anyone.

I want to be dead.

DECEMBER 28TH

When I got out after being hospitalised the first time, it only took a couple of days until I slipped up. And I didn't just slip up, I threatened mum with suicide. I stood in the kitchen, with the sharpest knife I'd been able to find and I'd held it to my arm. I remember her crying, begging me not to do it.

I did. Not the suicide, but I did cut myself on that knife.

We had a therapy session together today, and she mentioned that incident. How it crushed her, how it destroyed her, to see me so broken up. Over something that had been going on under her roof for all those years, and she hadn't noticed. How she just wanted to be able to help me.

I don't blame her. Maybe I did, when Andrew was

still a part of my life. But I don't anymore. She thought I was safe in his care. That I was being taken care of. No one thinks their husband would be capable of what he was capable of. He was my stepfather. Of course she would think he loved me like a son. She couldn't know how sick he really was.

But that incident... I don't want that to repeat itself. Not with Mum, and not with Damian. But I'm a ticking bomb. I can't say it won't happen, because it's very likely that it will.

Volatile. Mum used that word. That's what I am. She says she loves me despite of it. Damian says he loves me too, even if he hasn't actually said the word itself yet. I don't know what's keeping him back.

But I have to get better. Because I can't let myself fall so deep again. I don't want to die, not really. When things are dark and difficult, I might want it for a while. But it passes and then I want to be alive. I've got things to live for. People to live for. It would break them if I died.

That can't happen. I know what it's like to be broken. I can't do that to another person.

It's horrible — and it ruins your life.

CHAPTER 32

DAMIAN

I was changing out of my shirt and into my jumper when Spencer came into the back room.

"Thanks for covering for me," I told him as I hung my shirt up.

"No problem." Spencer smiled. "Josh's getting out today?"

I couldn't help the brief smile that flitted over my lips. "Yeah."

"Have a good day."

I grabbed my shoulder bag, nodded to Spencer and headed out.

Leslie was at the counter when I walked past. "Enjoy the rest of your day." He waggled his eyebrows at me, and I frowned in confusion until it dawned on me exactly what he meant.

Then I quickly turned away so he wouldn't see my face flush.

Josh was getting out, and I was getting off work early to be home when he was discharged, as we hadn't been together in over a month. Of course Leslie would think we'd be up to something dirty. How could he know we weren't? That we probably wouldn't ever be?

Silver and Kian were on the sofa when I got home.

"You're back." I stated the obvious.

Silver smirked at me. "Home sweet home."

They'd been staying away both for Christmas and New Years—with Kian's family. I'd been with my own, so I hadn't actually seen any of them in two weeks.

I went to my room to get rid of my shoulder bag. When I got back out again, they were bent over something on the table.

"Hey, D, come look at what Kian got me for Christmas."

I walked over slowly, not sure I wanted to know. They were pretty open about their relationship *and* their sex-life, and I wasn't sure I trusted any kind of gifts they'd give to each other.

It was probably something kinky that would totally embarrass me.

Except it wasn't.

Silver held up a ruby-coloured book. It had *Our Memories* printed on the front in gold, elegant writing.

"He got you a journal?" It was even fancier than the little leather-bound book I'd given Josh when we first met.

"Uh, no." Silver rolled his eyes as he handed it to me.

I glanced at them, just to make sure it was okay, and then flipped the cover open. The first page only had writing on it. Written with a gold marker on the ink-black papers. It was a personal message from Kian, with how much he enjoyed being with Silver, and that he loved him.

There was even a heart drawn after Silver's name. Another heart was drawn in front of Kian's name. It was cheesy and sappy, but also kind of sweet.

I flipped the page over again.

Kian had dedicated the double pages to the first month they'd been together. When I flipped the page again, the next two were dedicated to their second month together. So it continued for another two months. And then another two were devoted to January, but they only had a cut-in of a drawn image.

When I looked up at them again, Kian sat anxiously with his hands folded in front of the lower part of his face, like he was afraid of my reaction.

"This is quite... cheesy." I handed the book back to Silver. "But sweet. And nicely made." The four months they'd been together had been shown with pictures and handwritten text. It was like a scrapbook, of their progressing relationship.

"Maybe it gives you some ideas." Silver tilted the book towards me again before putting it down on the table.

"I think not. That's not exactly my style." If anything, it was more Josh's style. He was the one always writing in his journals.

"Doesn't hurt to be a bit romantic, you know." Silver stretched his arms out over the back of the sofa.

"I'm taking a shower." I locked myself in the bathroom. Being romantic wasn't really me, but there was one thing I could give Josh, that I knew he was waiting for.

Those words weren't something I'd grown up with.

It certainly hadn't been a part of our daily life when I was little, and Ray and Claire didn't go around spouting off the L-word whenever they felt like it.

I wasn't sure I'd ever heard them say it, in fact.

Once I was in the shower, I braced my arms against the wall and let the water beat down on me. I bowed my head down so I could look at my scar. It wasn't a pretty sight, the big, oblong line going down my torso. It was the result of a mad act by someone who was supposed to love me.

In the end she hadn't, which the scar was more than enough proof of.

Which the rest of my family's graves were proof of too.

But Josh deserved those words. More than that, he *needed* to hear them. I wanted him to be secure about me, about us, because if he wasn't things would continue to be precarious. I wanted him to feel as loved as possible, because I *did* love him.

I had to say the words to him. Today. It would be the first time I'd say them. And it would be to him.

He really was my first everything.

CHAPTER 33

J stood back to wait once I'd knocked on the door.

I wasn't sure why I was nervous. Maybe because I hadn't seen him for a few days. I just needed to see him. And tell him—

The door opened and he stood there, blue eyes taking me in in surprise. "I didn't know you were getting out this early." He pushed the door open wider.

"Happy belated birthday." I stepped into his personal space to kiss his cheek. "I'm sorry I haven't got you anything, but I came right over here once I was discharged."

"That's okay." His arms wrapped around me, all strong and safe. "You being here is enough."

We hugged for a long time, neither of us saying a word as we did so. When he finally let me go, and I got to enter the flat, my nervousness came back full-force.

"We need to talk."

He nodded and motioned for me to sit on the sofa. I did, though I perched at the end of my seat in my current anxiety. He sat down next to me, but with distance between us, so we weren't touching. He regarded me carefully.

"I'm not magically cured now or anything."

"I know that." His eyes narrowed a bit. "I know a month of hospitalisation isn't going to cure you."

"This is my life. This is how it's going to be for a long time. Maybe forever." I spread my hand out over my chest. I felt my heart beat quickly. "The cutting, and the mood swings, and the fear and the anxiety and the hospitalisations... it's going to be a part of my life. I'm not kidding myself into believing I won't need to be hospitalised again. Because I will. Because my mind is broken and scarred and it'll never heal properly."

"I know all of this, Josh." He leant forward, arms resting against his knees. "I know."

"I just want to make sure you know exactly what's ahead if you stay with me. I don't want to lose you. I can't lose you."

"You won't." He looked up at me. He seemed sincere. "I'm not the one struggling with impulsive actions. That's *you*. It's more likely that you'll leave me. I'm afraid I'll say one wrong word and your feelings about me will switch from good to bad. Borderliners are known to quickly fall in and out of love."

Love.

He'd said the word, even if he hadn't said it in the way I wanted to hear it.

"I know. I *know*." I gripped my shirt. I could still feel my heart beating wildly. "I ran away once. I can't promise that won't happen again either. But I'll always come *back*. I can't stay away from you. You're etched into my mind, like every shitty thing that's happened to me, but you're the one good part in it. The third degree burns on my mind analogy... you're like that too. You're etched into my mind along with everything else. But unlike all the bad, that's good. I haven't shared a bed with you in one month and six days. And in that timespan there haven't been many nights I've had a proper, good sleep. Whereas when I stay here with you, the good nights happen more often than the bad ones."

He was silent as he digested everything I'd just rambled off.

"I honestly believe," he said, staring straight ahead of him instead of at me, "that you're it for me.

I don't know how or why that happened, because I'm not the kind of person to get attached. But I did, to you, and it's done. It can't be undone. Whatever you do, Josh, whatever happens, I'll always be here. I'm not going anywhere. I can't. Because you made an impression on me. You etched yourself in my mind too—and now I can't get you out. I don't want to. All I want is to be with you, and I'll take anything you have to give."

"I have so much to give." I moved in closer to him, so that our thighs were touching. "I do. But I'm always going to be borderline, and there will be times I won't be around to give it."

"I don't care. As long as you'll always be back to give it, I'll always be waiting."

I stared into his blue eyes, taken aback by the intensity in his voice. I drew in a shaky breath. "What did I do to deserve you?"

He sat up straight. "Hey, Josh?"

"Yeah?"

He leaned in close. His hands came up to cup my cheeks, his thumbs stroking my cheekbones.

We stared into each other's eyes, though I felt a bit cross-eyed with how close we were.

"Yeah?" I repeated, the word coming out more as a breath.

"I love you." He kissed me then, and for that one, perfect moment, all was right in the world.

JANUARY 4TH

He said it. The words. The three big words. I love you.

I didn't known true happiness until that moment. That one, special perfect moment. And I believe his words. As long as I'll always come back to give, he'll always be waiting.

And I will—I always will be back.

How could I ever stay away?

ABOUT THE AUTHOR

TT lives in Norway and writes about gay men living in Norway. She also occasionally writes about gay men living in the UK, because she loves the UK. Norway might be too cold for her, but TT doesn't like the summer, so she's learned to adapt. TT is happiest in front of her computer, creating emotional stories about men loving other men.

www.ttkove.com
ttkove@gmail.com